I'd better get on with putting this on to tape; the story I have come back to record. I've been making notes for weeks, jotting down the thing I remember—the conversations, the impressions I had at the time—just so I could do this. Make this tape. Tell you these things in my own voice.

I'm doing it in the hope that someone will listen and realize that everything has changed.

Changed forever.

That the world they are living in is not the one it has always been. That there are a few of us left who can remember the way things were—the way they were meant to be.

HUMAN.4

MIKE A. LANCASTER

SCHOLASTIC INC.

First published in the United Kingdom by Egmont UK Limited, 2011

ISBN 978-0-545-51583-2

12 11 10 9 8 7 6 5 4 3 2 1   13 14 15 16 17 18/0

Printed in the U.S.A.   40

First Scholastic printing, January 2013

Book design by Room39b

To the girl in Cromwell that
I fell in love with and
who I am proud to call my wife.

"We are all in a post-hypnotic trance
induced in early infancy."
—R. D. Laing

"Is all that we see or seem
But a dream within a dream?"
—Edgar Allan Poe

"History doesn't repeat itself, but it rhymes."
—attributed to Mark Twain

HUMAN.4

WARNING:

THIS DATA STORAGE UNIT, OR "BOOK,"
HAS BEEN DESIGNED TO REPROGRAM
THE HUMAN BRAIN, ALLOWING IT TO
REPLICATE THE LOST ART THAT WAS ONCE
CALLED READING. IT IS A SIMPLE
ADJUSTMENT AND THERE WILL BE
NO NEGATIVE OR HARMFUL EFFECTS
FROM THIS PROCESS.

WHAT YOU ARE DOING:
"READING" EXPLAINED

EACH SHEET IS INDELIBLY PRINTED
WITH INFORMATION AND THE SHEETS
ARE VISUALLY SCANNED FROM LEFT TO
RIGHT, AND FROM TOP TO BOTTOM.

THIS SCANNED INFORMATION IS PASSED
THROUGH THE VISUAL CORTEX
DIRECTLY INTO THE BRAIN,
WHERE IT CAN THEN BE ACCESSED
JUST LIKE ANY OTHER DATA.

EDITOR'S NOTE

When Danny Birnie told us that he had hypnotized his sister we all thought he was mad.

Or lying.

Or both.

These are the words that begin the spoken narrative of Kyle Straker. It's a story that many have heard *about*, but few have had the opportunity to *hear* for themselves. It is both a piece of oral history from a time we are largely unfamiliar with—the early twenty-first century—and a tale with dark depths that, if true, has important lessons for us all to take away from it.

For those unfamiliar with the history of the Kyle Straker tapes, a brief recap might be helpful. The tapes were discovered two years ago, in the under-stair cupboard of a house in the small Cambridgeshire village of Millgrove. The first tape was labeled DIRE STRAITS. Luckily, the finder was an antique music enthusiast, who had the necessary analog equipment to play back the tapes, otherwise the story of Kyle Straker would have been condemned to the dustbin of lost history.

After discovering their true contents, the tapes were passed on to the authorities. They have been the subject of much controversy and debate ever since.

The peculiar format that you are holding— a book—was still the dominant form of information storage at the time the tapes were made. There is a reason that I insisted on this archaic format that will, I hope, become apparent as the narrative progresses.

If the story you are about to read is true, then this work is respectfully dedicated to the 0.4.

Mike A. Lancaster,
Editor

KYLE STRAKER'S FIRST TAPE

. . . Is this thing on?

Testing testing.

One two. One two. Two.

Ha. You know those roadies who get up onstage and test all the band's gear before a gig? And they do all that "testing testing, one two, one two" stuff into the microphones, to make sure they'll work when the singer finally takes the stage. Well, Simon once said that the reason they said "one two, one two" was because roadies couldn't count to three.

Made me laugh, but I guess you had to be there.

Anyway—how can you tell if these things are even working?

I mean, low tech or what?

Still, of course it's low tech, it's a tape recorder. An old and battered relic of a time before digital storage and CDs; iPods and MP3s; memory sticks and SD cards.

At least it works. I wasn't sure it would, it had been abandoned and left to rot in the cupboard under the stairs.

I kinda know how it feels.

Anyway, the tape player is old—it was made by Amstrad, the company started by that rude bloke off The Apprentice. *Mum used to love that show. Even went through a phase of saying "You're fired" for a while when we did something stupid or naughty.*

Funny the things you miss.

NOTE—*"The Apprentice"*

What was known—ironically as—"reality TV." Entwistle, in his paper "Manufacturing Nothing—Light Entertainment," writes: "Afraid to see the world around them as a larger picture, people instead reduced their views of the world to the tiny, artificial windows they called 'reality TV.' What is certain, however, is that reality played little or no part in such programs."

Oh, well. I'd better get on with putting this on to tape; the story I have come back home to record. I've been making notes for weeks, jotting down the things I remember—the conversations, the impressions I had at the time—just so I could do this. Make this tape. Tell you these things in my own voice.

I'm doing it in the hope that someone will listen and realize that everything has changed.

Changed forever.

That the world they are living in is not the one it has always been. That there are a few of us left who can remember the way things were—the way they were meant to be.

Looking back is easy, but there's a temptation to fill in blanks. I'm going to try to tell it as it happened to me, all in the right order and everything, without filling in any of the stuff I learned later. That's why my notes are going to be important.

I even know the way the story starts, the very moment it all started to change. The crazy thing that Danny said, that summer afternoon.

And, yes, Dad, I'm taping over one of your Dire Straits albums. Something you should have done a long time ago.

CHAPTER 1

When Danny Birnie told us that he had hypnotized his sister we all thought he was mad.

Or lying.

Or both.

The sister in question is a couple of years older than him and never struck me as the kind of girl who'd fall for any of Danny's nonsense.

She had to be used to it.

She lived with him.

So she had seen through his short-lived preoccupations with stamp collecting, and through the difficult withdrawal from his Pokémon addiction. She was even used to his new obsession with becoming the next David Blaine, and the hours he spent practicing with packs of cards.

She always struck me as the kind of girl who's going to be

a star. Some people are just like that. You know that they will, as my granddad used to say, land butter-side up.

There was no way that Danny—who, no matter how hard he tried, would always end up butter-side down—could have done what he had told us he had.

Danny's face was pale and thin, with dark semicircles under each eye, and his hair was a dirty-brown color, tousled on top. He was small for his age. Heck, it was my age too—and that's fifteen and a half, thanks for asking—and I was almost a full head taller than him. And he seemed to exaggerate that smallness by hunching his shoulders and bending his back.

"You should have seen it," he said, his eyes sparkling with excitement. "It actually worked. I mean, I knew it *could* work, but still, I didn't really think it *would*."

He ignored our disbelieving looks.

"I got her to relax. And I guided her into a hypnotic state. I didn't even need to say 'sleep' like they do on the telly. As I relaxed her, her eyes closed and her body went . . . sort of floppy. I hadn't even thought about what I'd get her to do when she *was* hypnotized, to be honest. So I told her that she was late for school—it was well past eight in the evening—and suddenly she flew into a panic, running around, throwing stuff into her school bag, and complaining about the alarm clock not waking her up."

He shook his head.

"It was priceless," he said.

He waited for one of us to say something.

And waited.

There was just me, Simon McCormack, Lilly Dartington, and Danny. We all lived down the same road in the small village of Millgrove, and we're all roughly the same age, so we tended to hang out together.

We were in "the shed," the bus shelter that squats by the side of the village green, and it was one of those long, hazy summer days that seem to stretch out into something closer to a week. To local kids, the shed was a place to meet up, hang out, practice some inept graffiti, and generally waste some time.

Across the green from the shed was the Methodist church, and next to that the combined infants and junior school that we all went to before moving to secondary school in the next village over, Crowley.

NOTE—*the "Methodist Church"*

A church was a building for the safe containment of primitive religious rites.

There was not a whole lot to do in Millgrove.

We couldn't get high-speed broadband yet and we were in the middle of a mobile-phone dead spot, which meant you couldn't get a signal within the village itself. We were one of the last generations in the country who didn't rely on mobile phones, although there were rumors that a new mast was going to help us catch up to the rest of the twenty-first century one day soon.

There was a tiny playing field where the older kids tried out smoking and train for future binge drinking, so we tended to avoid that. Then there were the three shops— a Happy Shopper, a family butcher shop, and a newsagent.

NOTE—*"Happy Shopper"*

A retail outlet whose name demonstrates the period's love of oxymorons—phrases that contain contradictory terms. Other examples are: "civil war," "reality TV," "constant change," "military intelligence," and "friendly fire."

The shed was pretty much in the center of the village, near enough to the shops in case we needed supplies, and it had a roof in case of English summer rain.

Simon and I had been friends for years. In all honesty I can't even remember how our friendship came about. Sure, we had a lot of the same interests and attitudes about things, but all that came later . . . I mean, it was revealed over time, so there must just be some . . . I don't know . . . *instinct* for friendship that's separate, somehow, from all of that.

Without the friendship, we'd never have discovered the reason we were friends.

You can drive yourself mad going round in paradoxical circles like that.

Simon and Lilly had been going out with each other for

a while now, and seeing as Simon was my best friend, I got pulled along with them a lot these days. It was weird getting used to sharing a friend . . . and . . . well, Lilly and I weren't getting on that well if the truth be told.

Danny lived next door to me and kind of just clings on to my coattails. Again, I don't know exactly why. Simon and I made him the butt of a lot of jokes but he just shrugged it all off.

That day we were just trying to fill up the day while using as little energy as we could.

And then, of course, Danny told us that he had hypnotized his sister.

Simon stared at him with a disbelieving look that summed up how the rest of us felt about Danny's revelation.

"You hypnotized Annette?" he said, and the spare disbelief he hadn't managed to put into his stare was crammed into the scathing way he said those three words. There was even a snort at the end of it.

Danny seemed to miss the incredulity and nodded.

"I've been reading a lot of books on the subject," Danny said, "and I've been watching lots of Paul McKenna and Derren Brown on DVD. With the talent show coming up I thought I might ditch the magic act this year and do a bit of stage hypnotism. You know, make people bark like dogs, or eat an onion as if it's an apple."

Simon groaned.

Of all of the area's customs and traditions, the Millgrove

talent show was by far the oddest. Every summer since Queen Victoria was sitting on the British throne—with a two-year gap during the Second World War—the people of Millgrove had gathered on the green to compete in the competition. Even when local lads were dying in the trenches in the First World War, the tradition continued.

Local folklore says the talent show began because of a dispute between two farmers, who'd fallen out over a woman and needed some way to settle the matter. Rather than firing pistols at each other, they each wrote a song for the girl and performed it on the green in front of the entire village, who were the judges of the competition. The village might have forgotten the men's names, but a version of their way of settling the argument was resurrected over a hundred years ago and still continued.

The talent show.

Weeks, even months in some extreme cases, were spent preparing acts (and I'm using that term loosely, most of them were lame karaoke offerings to amateur-sounding backing tracks) for the grand prize—a battered old cup and some WHSmith gift tokens. As long as it was a slow news week, there was a chance of a feature about the show in the *Cambridge Evening News*, with the winners grinning at the camera, holding their prizes.

Who was it who said something about everyone having their fifteen minutes of fame?

In Millgrove it was more like fifteen seconds.

To me the talent show had always been a bit of a cringe, really. When I was eight years old, my dad told that me that, as I was always cracking jokes and making people laugh, I should have a go at being a stand-up comedian at the show.

NOTE—*"Cracking Jokes"*

Humor was, according to Andrea Quirtell, an important coping mechanism for the horrors of the age. Some people actually counted "comedian" (or "joke teller") as their trade.

Quirtell identifies a number of different types of joke. There are: "puns" (which confuse the meanings of words for humorous intent), jokes that work only when written, jokes that appear in the form of a question, jokes that rely on bizarre or ambiguous language.

Immanuel Kant believed that people laughed at constructions like these because "(L)aughter is an effect that arises if a tense expectation is transformed into nothing." Quirtell disagrees. "Laughter is an effect that arises if a race refuses to grow up," she writes.

All in all they were the most embarrassing minutes of my life so far, even beating the moments Mum spent getting out the baby photographs the first time I brought a girlfriend (Katy Wallace, it lasted three weeks) home to meet the folks.

I discovered that there is a huge difference between knowing a few jokes and being a stand-up comic. I don't think I got a single gag right. I fluffed a punch line early on and then made a mistake in the setup of the next joke that made its punch line irrelevant. Sweating on the makeshift stage, with hundreds of faces staring at me, I dried up and just looked out at them in the grip of a huge panic attack.

I haven't entered the talent show since.

I rarely dragged myself along for it, if I'm honest. I always seemed to find something else to do. Like pairing socks, or cataloging my comics.

You know, important stuff.

"You *will* come and watch?" Danny asked, and there was a note of something close to desperation in his voice. "You will, won't you?"

"Well, I wouldn't miss it for the world," Lilly said, finally dragging her gaze away from the area of Simon's neck it had been focused on for most of Danny's "I'm a hypnotist" revelation.

I nodded.

A part of me even wanted to see Danny do well. To knock 'em dead. Become the talk of the village. Maybe even get his picture in the *Cambridge Evening News*.

But there was another part of me—and I'm not proud of this—that actually wanted to see him fail.

Miserably, horribly, and painfully.

It would be like exorcising a ghost.

It would be like therapy.

"Sure," I said, "I'll be there."

Lilly looked at me oddly, and a strange expression passed

across her face, like a cloud across the sun. I had a sudden sense of discomfort, as if Lilly had seen—or maybe felt—something that I should have seen or felt but didn't.

I raised an eyebrow to query it, but Lilly looked away, leaving me feeling foolish and confused.

Foolish, confused, and *something else*.

A dark sense of foreboding, as if a storm were brewing.

CHAPTER 2

That night—one of the last nights of my ordinary life—I mentioned Danny's intentions to my parents over the dinner table.

"Good on him," my dad said around a mouthful of vegetarian stew. "We haven't had a hypnotist before."

NOTE—*"Vegetarian Stew"*

Apparently "vegetarian" was still a dietary choice in Straker's day, rather than a social responsibility. See Chadwick's informative history: What Didn't They Eat? Flesh as Food.

Of course we haven't, I thought. *Who, apart from someone as mad as Danny, would suddenly decide they were going to become one?*

"It should make a nice change," he continued, looking at something on his fork with suspicion. A lump of beef-style Quorn stared back at him. "It's going to be great this year."

Yeah, great, I thought.

I could already pencil in a few of the high spots.

Mr. Bodean and his trombone.

Those creepy Kintner twins and their version of "Old Shep" that I'm sure was used in Guantánamo Bay to get Al Qaeda terrorists to talk.

Mr. Peterson, the village postman, and his annual ventriloquism act with a hideous homemade dummy called Mr. Peebles.

A whole bunch of hyperactive kids doing bad impersonations of Britney or Kylie or—*shudder*—Coldplay.

NOTE—*"Coldplay"*

O'Brien makes a persuasive case for defining "Coldplay" as referring to a kind of dramatic or musical presentation characterized by being utterly bereft of any signs of genuine emotion.

A recorder recital.

Some truly mind-numbing dance routines.

I shook my head.

Poor Danny.

"Are you going to be doing a turn this year?" my mum suddenly asked me. She actually wasn't joking, although it could easily be mistaken for some kind of sick humor.

I felt the usual prickle of shame pass from my stomach, up my spine, and onto my face where it magically made my cheeks go red.

"I don't think so," I said quietly, and prodded some

semicircles of carrot onto the far side of my plate with my fork.

Just let it go, I prayed silently, *please just let it go.*

No such luck.

"He's scared he'll choke again," said my idiot little brother, Chris, grinning.

I scowled at him.

"Christopher Straker!" Mum said sternly.

With Mum, full name equaled big trouble.

Chris's goofy grin fell from his lips.

"Well, he did choke," he muttered, trying to defend his comment by rephrasing it slightly.

Mum growled.

Dad, it seemed, was utterly oblivious to the exchange and was still thinking about Danny's star turn.

"I've always wondered how stage hypnotists get people to do all those things," he said. "I mean, it has to be some kind of trick, hasn't it? The people can't really be hypnotized, can they?"

"I'm sure I don't know," Mum offered. "Wasn't there a man who was hypnotized and then died and carried on living because no one had given him the command to wake up?"

"That was a film, dear," Dad said.

"It was a story by Edgar Allan Poe," I offered.

"I didn't know the Teletubbies *had* first names," Mum said, and I rolled my eyes at her.

"Danny says he hypnotized Annette," I said. "Made her think she was late for school."

Mum screwed up her face. "That was a bit mean of him," she said.

"*Was* she late for school?" my dad asked, missing the point, as usual, by about twenty-five meters.

Chris pulled a face at me, but I turned the other cheek and ignored him.

"The point is that she *must* have been hypnotized," I said.

Blank looks from Mum and Dad said I needed to explain a little further.

"It's the *summer holidays*," I said. "You don't get ready for school when there's no school to go to."

"Oh, yeah," Dad said.

"And it was nighttime," I finished.

Mum was looking over at Dad with one of the strange expressions that had become all too frequent in our house.

Even the simplest, most innocent statements could be met with tension, with Mum and Dad always on the lookout for traps and pitfalls in everything said within the walls of the house.

Because, I guess, they spent so much of their time setting them for each other.

This is a portrait of the Straker family *before* the talent show.

So, when things get crazy, you have a suitable base for comparison.

You see, Mum and Dad were "having problems," and were "trying to make a go of things." Both of those phrases, it turns out, are a sort of grown-up code for "their marriage was in trouble."

My dad had left us almost a year before, and he'd only come back a couple of months ago.

Anyway, to make a long story not quite so long, Mum couldn't cope when he was away. And so I stepped in to help her. I became the honorary "man" of the family, with responsibilities that I really didn't want or need placed upon my shoulders.

I ended up being responsible for Chris an awful lot.

Which meant I ended up telling Chris off an awful lot.

It wasn't something that sat very easily with me.

It certainly didn't sit very easily with him.

Mum was too emotionally drained to do battle with Chris, so it fell to me to make sure he did his homework, cleaned up his room, ate everything on his plate.

I became a miniature dictator.

I might have been helping Mum, but I sure as heck wasn't helping myself.

Or Chris, for that matter.

Things had been weird ever since he moved back in.

Every silence, action, or look held hidden meanings.

And I suddenly wasn't so important anymore. I went back to being a kid again. Any power I had assumed was gone in an instant.

I had been forced into a role that I didn't want, so why should I feel bitter about being squeezed out again?

Powerlessness, I guess.

Chris doesn't let me forget.

He resents any attention our parents offer me, and rejoices in seeing me fail.

Mum and Dad act as if nothing has changed, when even I can see everything has.

That's my family.

Drives you absolutely crazy.

But you miss them when they're no longer here.

When the bad stuff comes—and it always will—you look back on those moments with longing.

The bad stuff was just around the corner.

The talent show changed everything.

Forever.

That's why I like to think about the way things were, however imperfect they seemed at the time.

In extraordinary times, the ordinary takes on a glow all of its own.

CHAPTER 3

The talent show loomed.

Danny kind of dropped off the radar and Simon joked that it wasn't as if he was sitting in his room practicing by himself—surely a hypnotist needed people to practice *on*.

A few days before the show, Dad even toyed with the idea of entering the show himself, announcing that his Elvis impersonation "wasn't half bad." Good sense prevailed when Mum pointed out it wasn't "half bad" because it was "completely awful." He sulked a bit, but I reckon he was a little bit relieved when the original bravado had worn off.

The day of the show arrived and people got up just as they always had. They went shopping. They cleaned their cars. They read newspapers. They gossiped over garden fences.

They made their way to the green.

Simon, Lilly, and I were near the back, cross-legged on the grass, drinking reasonably cold Cokes from the Happy

Shopper, and watching Mr. Peterson's act with something close to horror.

Mr. Peebles was even more hideous than I remembered.

A grotesque papier-mâché head, like a dried-up orange, sat on top of a square, unnatural-looking body. The dummy's eyes *sort of* moved about—they were actually little more than very poorly painted Ping-Pong balls—but they only went from one impossible cross-eyed position to another.

Every time Mr. Peterson operated the thing's mouth there was this horrible, hollow knocking sound that was often louder than the thin, falsetto voice that was supposed to come from Mr. Peebles.

To call Mr. Peterson a "ventriloquist" is to insult the profession because there was no art to what he did. It implies that his lips didn't move and there was at least an *illusion* that it was the dummy doing the talking.

Not Mr. Peterson.

Mr. Peterson's lips *always* moved.

They moved when he was doing his straight-man routine as himself, and they seemed to move *even more* when he was speaking for his dummy.

But that was only the beginning of his lack of talent.

Every letter *B* was guaranteed to sound like a *G*. Every *M* became a tortured *N*. The letter *F* was a horrible *Th* sound. *P* was replaced with a *Cl* that made it sound like Mr. Peterson had a ball of hair in his throat. *W* was an unconvincing *Ooh*.

To be brutally honest, I don't think Mr. Peterson ever

practiced. Between one talent show and another I think Mr. Peebles went back into his box and stayed there.

And the weird thing is that, at no point in the proceedings did Mr. Peterson seem to draw any pleasure from his own act. He looked, by turns, utterly terrified, and on the brink of tears: as if this wasn't entertainment but some strange kind of punishment he was putting himself through.

Year after year.

He stood there, sweating in the heat of the afternoon sun—the body of Mr. Peebles hanging limply from his hand—wearing the wide-eyed look of a rabbit dazzled by headlights.

"What's up, Mr. Peebles?" he said. "You look sad."

The head of the dummy swiveled through so many degrees that it would have broken a real creature's neck.

"I get you don't really care ooh-ats wrong with ne," came the reply.

"Of course I care, Mr. Peebles. Now, what's wrong?"

"I've groken ny gicycle."

Mr. Peterson tried to move the dummy's head, and then spent a couple of seconds trying to stop the head from falling off.

The smaller kids were chuckling and occasionally roaring with laughter.

"It's like a traffic accident," Simon whispered to me. "It's horrible, and wrong, but you can't take your eyes off it."

"The act?" I asked. "Or the whole thing?"

Lilly leaned forwards. "You know that show, *Britain's Got Talent?*" she asked.

NOTE—*"Britain's Got Talent"*

One imagines a televised version of the talent show that Kyle is describing.

In "Stars in Their Lives," Reg Channard writes: "The obsession with celebrity was an all-consuming illness that had reached epidemic proportions by the early years of the twenty-first century. Adolescents actually stopped studying at schools and colleges in favor of the pursuit of this crazy fever dream of celebrity. The end result was that many menial, degrading jobs were taken by people who possessed no formal qualifications, but had reasonable singing voices and knew a couple of poorly choreographed dance routines."

I nodded.

"They lied," she said.

Mr. Peterson stumbled on for a few more minutes that felt much longer, before he took his applause and shuffled offstage.

The show's host—Eddie Crichton, who ran the village's sports and social club—wandered onto the stage looking mildly baffled.

"Er . . . well . . . um . . . ," he said, possibly trying to work out how year after year Mr. Peterson failed to improve his act. "Now, a little bit of a change from the ordinary." He was regaining enthusiasm now. "As we set off on a voyage into the mysteries of the human mind. I'd like to hear a big Millgrove welcome for . . . THE GREAT DANIELINI!"

Simon nudged me in the ribs, really hard, and raised his eyebrows.

"Danielini?" he whispered. "What kind of name is that?"

"Not a particularly good one," I whispered back.

I looked around at the people watching, acutely aware of just how badly this could all go for Danny if his act didn't match up to the billing he'd just been given.

I could see Danny's mum a couple of rows forwards of us watching the whole thing through the viewfinder of a tiny camcorder. I remember thinking how cruel it was to be filming him, and how at least I had been spared the humiliation of having my own talent show appearance filmed by my parents.

For some reason I had a sudden urge to check the crowd for Danny's sister, but I couldn't see her anywhere.

Maybe she was sensible and had found something more fun to do.

Like hammering nails into her feet.

Then Danny stepped onto the stage.

CHAPTER 4

You know, sometimes you see a person you know, but there's something different about them and you have to look again—do a double take—because you're suddenly not certain it's the person you thought it was. Maybe it's a haircut that makes you suddenly uncertain, or a look on their face that you've never seen there before.

And often you're absolutely right, it's not who you thought it was, it's just someone who looks a *little* like them and you're relieved that you didn't call out their name.

Or feel like a total ass because you did.

When Danny walked out I had the same thing happen inside my brain. I mean, I knew it was Danny, but then I doubted it and had to look again.

It wasn't just that he'd got himself a smart dinner suit that actually fit him—although that helped. It wasn't that his usually random-angled hair had been gelled and slicked back—although that helped too.

It was something that was both of those things, plus something else.

"He looks *older*," Lilly said almost breathlessly, and Simon laughed at her comment.

He was wrong to laugh.

It was true.

Danny did look older.

Taller, too, because he'd lost his habitual slump.

And his face had an intensity to it that made him look a whole lot wiser than the kid who was the constant butt of our stupid jokes.

He stood in the middle of the stage as helpers lined up four chairs behind him. He was looking out across the audience with an confident expression that seemed almost spooky on a kid his age, almost as if we were seeing a glimpse of Danny as he was going to be, twenty or so years in the future.

"Good afternoon," he said calmly and commandingly. "Welcome to my demonstration of the powers of the human mind."

He unbuttoned his jacket and reached into the inside breast pocket, pulling out a brand-new deck of cards. He took them from their box, cracked the seal and removed the cellophane, then mixed them up with a series of overhand shuffles.

Danny was a master with a pack of cards—he practiced card magic in front of his bedroom mirror—and I was suddenly afraid that he had chickened out of his hypnotism act in favor of some more of what he'd been doing at the talent show for the last couple of years.

"A deck of cards, new and shuffled," he said, squaring the deck in his hands. "But I only require nineteen of them."

He counted off the top nineteen cards and threw the rest over his shoulder.

"Although, actually, it's not really nineteen cards that I require," he said, fanning the cards out in front of him so that we could only see their backs. "I need something else. Only the cards can tell me what."

He continued to fan them out, and then turned them around to the audience with a flourish.

Instead of the usual hearts, clubs, diamonds, and spades there was a single letter on each card. Danny had fanned them out in such a way that there were gaps between certain cards that made the word breaks in the sentence the cards spelled out.

The cards read: I NEED FOUR VOLUNTEERS.

"Ah," Danny said as if the cards had just solved a difficult problem for him. "I guess I need four volunteers. Any takers?"

CHAPTER 5

It was a good trick.

Actually it was an *impressive* trick, and I know some of the sleight of hand and false shuffles that Danny used to do it.

The rest of the audience thought it was pretty cool too. There was a round of applause.

At the end of it, no one had their hand up.

Danny was looking out across the sea of faces, but there were no takers.

Moments passed and still no one volunteered. It felt like the longer it went on, the less likely he was to get someone to put their hand up. I realized that I was gritting my teeth and holding my breath.

And still Danny looked around the audience, and there was a moment in which the stage persona seemed on the brink of slipping.

No Danny, I thought, *don't ruin it.*

It was only then that I realized my hand had raised itself up above my head. I had been thinking about how maybe I should put it up, but I hadn't got much past the initial thought, and certainly hadn't reached a proper decision yet.

To this day I can't remember lifting my hand up.

Danny saw it and the calm returned to his features.

"Ladies and gentlemen, we have *two* volunteers," he said, and that threw me. He was looking over at me and gesturing for me to join him onstage.

Then I caught a movement out of the corner of my eye and realized that Lilly had her hand up too.

She caught my eye, smiled an odd kind of smile, and then shrugged.

If I'd known Lilly was going to stick her hand up, I'd never have volunteered. I only put it up because I thought it might, you know, spare a friend some embarrassment.

Still, it was too late now. I couldn't put my hand down and pretend it had never gone up.

I saw Simon looking at me with a look like I'd grown an extra head or something.

"That's two people my own age," Danny said as Lilly and I made our way to the front. "How about a couple of brave adults to make up the numbers?"

So there I was. There was Lilly. There was Mr. Peterson—

without Mr. Peebles. And there was Mrs. O'Donnell, a woman who served behind the counter at the Happy Shopper.

Four volunteers.

We stood there, in front of the whole village just about, and I reckon we were all wishing we had kept our hands firmly down at our sides.

I could see my parents in the crowd. My dad was smiling and pointing. He had his phone out and was taking a photo. That's all mobile phones are good for in Millgrove. I immediately felt self-conscious.

Danny went down the line of four and welcomed us onstage and then got us to sit on four chairs: Lilly, then me, then Mrs. O'Donnell, with Mr. Peterson at the end.

I felt awkward, and not just because this was the same stage I'd died on as a comedian, but simply because I was next to Lilly. There's . . . oh, it's complicated . . . an odd dynamic . . . er . . . Look, I'll leave this for now because I'm talking about Danny.

"I want you to answer me truthfully," he said to us, but it was clear that the performance was for the sake of the gathered crowd. "It's very important that the answers you give are absolutely honest. Can you do that?"

We sort of nodded and mumbled, unsure as to what Danny wanted.

"Good," he said. "Have I prepared any of you for this moment? Have I coached you or in any way influenced you?"

Shakes of heads and muttered "no"s.

"Okay. Thank you."

He turned to the audience.

"Now, what I'm going to attempt today is no less than the hypnosis of our subjects here." The statement caused a small buzz of excitement among the crowd. "While I haven't had the time to put our courageous volunteers into a deep hypnotic trance, I am going to try to relax them to the point where they can carry out a few . . . er . . . tasks for me, just to show that they are indeed in a suggestible state."

He smiled, suddenly seeming miles away from the gawky, socially useless kid I'd lived next door to all my life.

"Give me a couple of minutes, can you?" he asked the audience, then spun on his heel, came back to where we were sitting, and squatted in front of us.

"I want you to relax." His voice was quiet, mellow, soothing. "I want you to close your eyes and study the darkness you find there."

Okay, I thought, *I'll play along.*

I closed my eyes.

"Concentrate on my voice," Danny said. "Let it be your guide. You must not open your eyes until I tell you. If you understand me, nod your heads now."

I nodded. Already my head felt heavy. It stayed nodded down.

"Good." Danny's voice was even more soothing. "There

is so much weight inside your heads, too many thoughts. We need to let go of them. I want you to imagine that the darkness you are seeing now is the screen of a television set. All dark. Dark. Dark and empty.

"Now, imagine a ball of light in the center of the screen. It's bright. *Too* bright. It's a circle of light that is really, really bright at its center, but gets hazy towards the edges. *See* the ball of light. *See* the hazy edges. *See* the darkness that surrounds it. Imagine it precisely, and hold it in your mind. You *must* see it. You must see it clearly. You *can* see it. I know you can."

As he spoke, the image he wanted me to see settled into my mind. I saw it in perfect detail, could even see the hazy edges, and it *was* too bright.

Uncomfortably so.

"Now *concentrate*. Concentrate and let your body relax. Let your fingers relax, one by one. Notice that when you relax those fingers, the ball of light becomes dimmer. You are turning down the light just by relaxing your fingers. Relax them some more. Turn the brightness down some more."

I let my fingers relax. The light lost some of its brightness.

"Now I want you to start to relax your hands, let them become weightless. Watch the light dimming as you do it. Feel the relaxation spread to your arms, making them weightless. The light dims some more. It's all hazy now, that light, and as you relax it gets hazier. Let your body relax, let your mind become soothed by the light as it fades, relax your arms, your shoulders, your neck. Let your mind grow as dark as the screen, as the light fades, as your body relaxes. Let go of all the thoughts that are weighing you down."

I felt my mind do just that, letting go of all the baggage, all the chatter.

As the light faded out into perfect darkness I realized that Danny's voice was fading out with it.

It didn't seem odd; in fact, I welcomed the darkness.

Soon there was nothing else.

Just darkness.

And peace.

NOTE

The Parker experiment attempted to test Daniel Birnie's method of hypnosis using the exact words transcribed here. It was a total failure. Either Kyle Straker's memory or Birnie's method was flawed.

Peace, perfect peace.

I'd never realized that my head was so darned noisy, that thoughts and images and sounds are ringing around it constantly. You don't think of your head as being a particularly chaotic place to live.

I wasn't asleep, I knew that, but I must have been in a state pretty close to sleep.

I could still hear things *outside* my head, but I couldn't focus on them.

There's a difference between hearing something and listening to it.

It's kind of hard to say much more about the experience— soon I wasn't thinking, seeing, or hearing: I wasn't anything really.

As it turned out, however, it didn't last long and . . .

EDITOR'S NOTE

It seems that Kyle was as unfamiliar with old-fashioned tape recordings as people today would be. He was unaware of the blank beginning and end of an analog tape. As a result, when the tape switched off, he probably thought that his last few words had been captured, but they were not.

This is true of all three of the Straker tapes.

. . . *forgotten that tapes need turning over? How did they ever get to be a dominant technology? You don't turn a CD over—why would you split an album up into two halves?*

It's funny, all the ordinary stuff—the last of my ordinary stuff— all of it fitting on to one side of a cassette.

The next thing I remember . . .

CHAPTER 6

The next thing I remember is that I woke up.

Suddenly.

Pulled out of a state of peace and calm, I opened my eyes and for a few seconds I couldn't process anything and just sat there, waiting for my brain to start working properly again.

The world was a sickening Technicolor blur. I could see rows of blurry pink balloons that were, perhaps, faces. I could sense people around me, could hear sounds and feel people close to me, but it took a while for me to put everything together.

Then my vision kicked back in. The pink balls I had seen were the faces of the audience, staring up at me and the other people upon the stage.

I had a sudden feeling that something was different; that something had changed.

I looked around and saw that Lilly was opening her eyes. Her eyes looked . . . I don't know, almost *supernaturally* blue as they locked onto mine, and this weird half smile played across her lips. Then she broke eye contact, and her face kinda creased up with puzzlement.

I followed her eye line.

Danny was standing close by, watching us with a strange expression on *his* face.

It wasn't a look of confusion.

It was more like shock.

He was standing totally still, hands clenched into tight fists at his sides. He seemed frozen to the spot.

Completely immobile.

"What on earth is going on?" someone asked, and I followed the sound back to my right-hand side.

Mrs. O'Donnell was staring wide-eyed across the audience. Her pinched face looked alarmed. She was half out of her seat as if she had been trying to stand, something had stopped her, and she hadn't worked out what to do next.

And her face looked pale.

Very pale indeed.

"What is it?" I asked her. "What's wrong?"

Instead of answering she just pointed out into the crowd and I noticed her hand was shaking. I followed her finger and realized I was shaking too.

I felt my mind fighting to explain it away.

And failing.

Everyone in the audience was statue-still, frozen in their place just like Danny was. But they weren't just *still*: they were utterly motionless. And their faces were frozen in an expression exactly the same as Danny's. You know when you freeze frame a DVD and everything just stops until you press PLAY again? It was a lot like that, I guess.

One of my dad's favorite pictures is that weird one by Edvard Munch called *The Scream*. He's got a print of it in his study, and we used to joke that it was the real thing, back when the original got stolen. The painting shows a figure—you can't really tell if it's a man or a woman— standing on a bridge, in front of a blood-red sky. A couple of figures are watching in the background, but they're not important, the main focus is that figure in the foreground; hands on either side of its face, its mouth wide open.

I've looked at that picture more than a hundred times, hanging there over my dad's desk, and I have tried to figure out what is going on in that figure's head, to make it look so full of despair.

I still don't know, but I saw it imprinted across the faces of everyone in Millgrove.

Everyone except four, anyway.

I—I haven't got the words to describe how disturbing the sight was. Every one of those faces was gripped by some fear, or despair, that had literally frozen them to the spot. It was too unreal, too weird, and I turned away.

Mrs. O'Donnell had sat back down, and was gazing around her in snaps and jerks.

I felt a pressure on my arm and realized that Lilly had just grabbed hold of it as her eyes raked the scene, trying to understand what she was seeing. It felt . . . *good* . . . to have her reach out for me in that moment.

As I said earlier, strange dynamic.

Mr. Peterson's face had turned ashen and he was just staring ahead with his eyes bulging out of his head.

And then I got it.

It was a joke.

Something that Danny had told them all to do when we woke up, just to mess with our heads.

It was part of the act.

I laughed.

"Very funny, everyone," I said loudly. "You had us worried there."

No one moved. No one laughed. No one did anything but remain still.

I waited.

Nothing.

No joke then.

So what was going on?

CHAPTER 7

A weird kind of panic descended.

I mean, this was just plain freaky.

These were all people we knew; people we saw every day; people we had grown up with; said hi to if we saw them on the street.

But they weren't moving.

They weren't moving at all.

I'm not sure I've done this . . . *stillness* . . . justice yet. I mean, this wasn't people *pretending* to be still. You know, like when they play musical statues, or whatever, and they freeze, but not really.

The truth is, people can't stay still for long. Not without a whole lot of practice. Not this amount of people. Not for this long. Human bodies aren't built for inactivity. They sway. They smile. They move, even if it's only a little. They giggle.

None of the audience were doing any of these things.

It was eerie and unnatural.

Mrs. O'Donnell said, "I've had enough of this."

She got to her feet, stomped over to Danny, and pushed him very gently. He didn't offer any resistance. He moved, but in the way an inanimate object moves when pushed. He swayed slightly, then stopped. His face didn't change. Not a muscle of his body twitched.

Mrs. O'Donnell snapped her fingers in front of his face. He didn't react. He didn't even blink, and I realized that I hadn't seen any of the audience blink in all the time we had been awake.

I had a really bad feeling spreading through me, the kind that brings bumps of gooseflesh up on the skin of your arms. That makes the nape of your neck feel cold.

Mr. Peterson was sitting, rocking back and forwards, while his lips moved quickly in silent conversation with himself.

"What's wrong with *him*?" Lilly asked.

I shrugged.

"Shock, I guess," I said. "I sort of feel like sitting down and doing it myself."

I pointed out over the audience.

"The question we *ought* to be concentrating on is: what's wrong with *them*?"

Lilly took my arm again, and her fingers fixed tight this time.

"What about Simon?" she whispered.

"Let's go see," I said feeling disappointed. *How bad is that, by the way? To feel disappointed that she was concerned about my best friend?*

I led her from the stage and onto the green below.

Among the crowd, the level of weirdness was raised by a factor of ten.

Or twenty.

Down there, the effect was even more astonishing.

It was as if everyone had been switched off in the middle of whatever it was they were doing. Like the stopped mechanical exhibits you'd see at closing time in a museum, turned off in mid-motion.

People held canned drinks in the air. Kids had their hands in packets of crisps. Old man Davis was frozen in the midst of scratching his nose. Annie Bishop and her boyfriend, Nigel Something-or-other, were in the middle of a kiss. Ned Carter was looking up at the sky. Ursula Lincoln was coughing, with her hand up to her mouth.

About halfway to where we had left Simon, I found my mum and dad. They were just sitting there, totally still, my mum's finger pointing accusingly at my meek-looking dad. They had been arguing, and then they had just stopped.

There were only four of us outside of stopped time, and able to move around those that were frozen in it.

But it wasn't time that had stopped. Things were moving.

It was only the people that were stopped. There were flies buzzing around; wasps crawling around the drinking holes of soft-drink cans; clouds of midges swirling in the summer air. Birds still crossed the sky. A cool breeze blew, carrying candy wrappers and other discarded items. Mrs. Winifred's Italian greyhound, Bambi, was walking around looking lost.

Whatever this was, it seemed to affect only human beings.

All human beings except me, Lilly, Mrs. O'Donnell, and Mr. Peterson.

It was 100 percent weird.

"I'm scared," Lilly confessed.

"Me too." I smiled a tight-lipped smile. "But we've got to keep it together. There's an explanation for this. We've just got to find it."

"Well, I don't have an explanation," Lilly said, pouting. "Not a one. I mean this is impossible, you realize that, don't you? It's like one of those awful movies on the Sci Fi Channel. I really hate science fiction."

Standing there—looking afraid, with fear-wide eyes, dilated pupils, and all her usual defenses down—Lilly looked . . . well, really pretty.

It's something about her that she tries to hide, so I guess it's her way of staying out of things, by distancing herself from them. You don't get involved, you don't get let down, I guess.

Now, though, she looked different.

47

Her cheeks were flushed and her eyes sparked with life. No longer a disinterested observer, she had come to life.

Anyway, Simon was sitting in the exact same place we'd left him. His hands were folded in his lap and his face was frozen in the same openmouthed expression as the others.

Lilly touched Simon's face.

"He's warm," she said, moving her fingers to his neck. She held two fingers on the side of his neck, held them there trying to find a pulse, and then she smiled. "Still alive."

The relief in her voice was obvious.

I felt a harsh twinge of jealousy. Yeah, I know, not exactly an honorable reaction, and I'm not proud.

"If he's alive, there's hope," I offered, and Lilly's face brightened.

"But how do we wake them up?" she asked. "We were the ones who were supposed to be hypnotized. Did it go wrong? Did Danny hypnotize everyone else? Even *himself*?"

I was going to attempt an answer, when my train of thought was interrupted by a loud wailing sound behind us.

CHAPTER 8

Mr. Peterson had lost it.

Just seriously lost it.

When we got back to the stage we found him on his knees, head in his hands, making the horrible sound we'd heard. His face was red and his cheeks were wet with tears. His head was bowed, revealing a sunburnt bald spot in his graying hair.

Mrs. O'Donnell was bent over, trying to comfort him, but he thrashed her away with wild, windmill arms. There was spittle around his lips.

"What happened?" I asked her.

Mrs. O'Donnell shook her head.

"I don't know. He'd stopped the rocking and was sitting there in his seat, looking around. "And then this . . ."

Lilly approached him warily, keeping her distance in case those arms struck out again.

"Mr. Peterson?" she asked soothingly. "Can you tell us what is wrong?"

There was no reply, just an increase in the volume of Mr. Peterson's wailing. A thin, high-pitched noise that sounded more like the voice of Mr. Peebles than his own.

Suddenly, it hit me: how much trouble we were in. Everyone on the village green had been inexplicably, completely immobilized, by some force or sickness that we just couldn't guess. Only the four people who had been hypnotized as part of Danny's act remained unaffected by the event.

We were alone.

But where did that leave us? What could we do?

"We need to get help," I said. I turned to Mrs. O'Donnell. "The Happy Shopper is open today—how many people are working there?"

"Just Tony," she said. "Tony Jefferson. Shop manager. Everyone else is here."

"Let's go and see how *he* is," I said.

Mrs. O'Donnell tried to get Mr. Peterson onto his feet, but he wasn't having any of it. He just made that horrible wailing sound and then descended into tears. They were the kind of tears that made a person's whole body shake. Mrs. O'Donnell couldn't get close to him without him striking out at her.

"You two go," she said to Lilly and me. "Go and see if Tony's okay. I'll stay here and make sure Rodney doesn't do himself any harm."

"Rodney?"

Mrs. O'Donnell pointed to Mr. Peterson. I'd known him all my life and never knew his first name.

"Oh," I said. "Rodney."

"And I'm Kate," Mrs. O'Donnell said.

I gave her as close to a smile as I could manage, and nodded my head.

"We'll be back as soon as we can," I said.

Lilly and I made our way through the rows of stationary people, across the green, out onto the High Street, past the shed, and towards the Happy Shopper.

The High Street itself was deserted and strangely quiet. There were no cars driving down the road, which is, like, unheard of on a Saturday afternoon. Millgrove is a common alternative to the main highway and there is *always* traffic.

We hurried as fast as we could without actually breaking into a jog.

"What's causing this?" Lily asked me. "I mean, something's got to be doing it."

"I'm afraid that, in the words of a certain science teacher, 'We simply don't have enough data to form a conclusion.'" I used a rough approximation of Mr. Cruikshank's voice.

Lilly started to laugh, then seemed angry with herself for

showing humor in such bizarre circumstances. I thought there might be a large measure of guilt behind it: we were walking around while Simon was frozen to the spot.

"So where do we get more data?" she asked.

I pointed to the bright windows of the shop ahead.

"Here will be a start," I said.

The Happy Shopper was just like any other Happy Shopper anywhere on the planet.

Except smaller.

Millgrove didn't do anything big, except maybe that idiot talent show.

I pushed open the advert-papered shop door.

The bell above the door rang. It wasn't an electric buzzer or beeper; it was a genuine, old-fashioned brass bell.

I walked in with Lilly following close on my heels.

There were two other people in the shop: Tony Jefferson, standing behind the counter, and Eddie Beattie over by the drinks cooler.

Tony had been freeze-framed in the act of refilling one of the displays of Wrigley's gum that stood on the counter, strategically placed for those last-minute buys.

Eddie Beattie was choosing a can of high-impact cider from the fridge, and he looked like he'd just made up his mind and was reaching towards a shelf in the cooler when . . .

When whatever happened, happened.

Up until that moment I had been thinking that the state of the people on the green had something to do with Danny and his hypnosis. I know it wasn't a likely idea, but it was a lot more comforting than any other I could come up with.

But Tony and Eddie hadn't been present at the green.

Whatever this was, it wasn't restricted to the talent show audience.

"Is it just Millgrove?" Lilly's voice quavered. "Or is it the whole world?"

I shook my head.

"There's only one way to find out," I said.

I popped the catch on the shop counter, just like I'd seen the staff do for years, and I lifted the flap that let me in. I ignored Tony, located the radio he kept behind there, flicked the POWER button, and turned up the volume.

A harsh shriek of static tore through the still air.

"Sorry," I said, turning the volume down a few notches so the noise didn't *quite* hurt. Then I spun the tuning dial, searching the wavelengths and bands for a signal.

Any signal.

All I found were variations on the same general theme of earsplitting interference.

"Is it broken?" Lilly asked.

I tried to remember if it had been playing earlier when we'd stopped in for cold drinks, but if it had, it hadn't registered.

"I guess it could be," I said. "Or something could be jamming radio signals. Or, I suppose, I could be finding no stations because there *are* no stations out there to find. . . ."

Lilly's suddenly panicked face told me that maybe some of my ideas ought to remain inside my head, and not just thrown out at someone unprepared for them.

"Or maybe it's sunspot activity, electromagnetic storms, UFOs, or the well-planned revenge of the dolphins," I said, trying humor instead.

"How can you make jokes at a time like this?" Lilly demanded, and I felt about an inch and a half tall. "It's not as if you have a particularly good history as a comedian."

"Actually I'm just trying to find a way to deal with all this," I said. "I'm sorry if it sounds like I'm not taking things seriously, I honestly don't know what else to do."

"Simon keeps saying how immature you are," she said coldly.

I felt my cheeks get hot.

"Still," she added cruelly.

Lilly's words stung, and I blurted out, "What are you talking about?"

"Just what I said," she said. Then she looked down at her feet. "Look, can we not do this now?"

"You started it."

"See?" she said almost victoriously. "Immature. *You started it*," she whined.

I had a hundred things I could say on the tip of my tongue, all witty, devastating, and some of them were even true . . .

"I think I'll try the phone," I said instead.

CHAPTER 9

Run through the numbers you'd try in a situation like this one, and I bet the first one you'd dial is the same number I did.

Three digits.

999.

Emergency Services.

Didn't even ring.

I'd got a dial tone, but when I put the numbers into the keypad the phone just went dead. There was an empty, hollow silence. Then a few, ominous clicks on the line. Then more silence.

I tried another couple of numbers I knew—a friend in Crowley and another in Cambridge—and got nothing. I rang my own home phone. Nothing again. No line outside the village, no line inside.

I put the phone down.

"Well?" Lilly asked.

I shook my head.

"Phones are dead," I said.

"How is that possible?"

"I don't know. Maybe whatever this is stretches farther than Millgrove."

Lilly's face screwed up and for a moment I thought she was going to cry. I wouldn't have blamed her. I felt like crying myself. To her credit she pulled herself out of it before the tears actually started.

"So what do we do now?" she asked.

I shrugged, then realized that was a bit cold. It might sound a little self-absorbed, but Lilly's words about Simon thinking I'm immature kept ringing around in my head. Yeah, I know: way to turn a crisis of maybe global proportions into a bit of navel-gazing about whether my best friend really likes me.

I needed to rise above it.

Deep breath.

"We go back," I said. "Back to the green. There's got to be something there that can tell us what's happened."

Lilly didn't look convinced but she nodded.

We started towards the door. I grabbed a couple of cold cans of Red Bull from the fridge and left the exact change on the counter.

Lilly pointed up at the CCTV camera above the door. A red light shone below its lens.

"Maybe it can show us what happened," she said hopefully.

I shook my head.

"It's a dummy," I told her. "Danny helps out here, and he said it's not real. A shoplifting deterrent."

"Oh," Lilly said.

"Good idea, though," I said clumsily.

"Thanks," Lilly said.

An uneasy truce had perhaps been reached, just before a fight broke out.

And then we left the shop in silence.

When we got back to the green, it hadn't changed. I think that I had been hoping that things would be sorted out by the time we returned, that everyone would have started moving again and we could just forget all that had happened, laugh it off, and wait for a sensible explanation on TV later on.

Mrs. O'Donnell—it was still hard to think of her as Kate—looked like she'd aged about five years in the time we'd been away. She was usually a neat, forty-something woman with a sort of peroxide-bob hairstyle that made it look like she wished she was still in her thirties.

Or twenties, even.

Now her hair was messed up, her face was beaded with sweat, and frown lines plowed up her brow.

She was standing over the fetal form of Mr. Peterson and

was obviously losing patience with him. In fact, she seemed on the verge of delivering a kick to his backside.

She looked relieved to see Lilly and me, even when we shook our heads to show her we'd made no progress.

"He's been like this since you left," she said, pointing to the prone form of the ventriloquist. "You kids are handling this a whole lot better than he is."

I wondered if that meant that we were pretty darned tough.

Or whether we simply lacked the imagination to see how bad things really were.

We told Mrs. O'Donnell about our trip to the shop. She seemed especially disturbed by the fact the phones weren't working, but to be honest, I was too. It hinted at a problem that stretched farther than the village boundaries.

"We need a TV," Mrs. O'Donnell said. "The Internet. Anything that will give us a bigger picture."

"The radio and telephone don't work," Lilly reminded her.

"Doesn't mean that every form of communication is down," Mrs. O'Donnell said. "Come on."

"Where?" Lilly asked.

"My house."

"What about him?" I pointed to Mr. Peterson.

Mrs. O'Donnell shook her head.

"We'll have to come back for him," she said. "I can't get him to do anything but that."

"Let me try," I said.

She nodded.

I crouched down over the man. His eyes were squeezed as tight shut as eyes can be. His lips moved rapidly, but no sounds came out from between them.

"Mr. Peterson?" I said. "Can you hear me?"

If he could, he was making no visible signs.

"Mr. Peterson?" I touched his shoulder as I spoke and suddenly he let out a scream of terror. His eyes shot open like the eyes of a china doll. They met mine and for an instant he looked perfectly sane and rational.

"Are you all right, Mr. Peterson?" I said.

His eyes were wide, but he looked like he was back with us.

"Everything . . . it's all changed," he said so quietly I had to move my ear closer to his lips to hear.

"What do you mean?" I asked him.

His voice got louder, stronger.

"They're gone," he said. "Changed. All of them. You hear me? *I . . . I SEE THEM!*"

His words sent a physical chill down my spine.

"See what?" I demanded. "What can you see?"

"All of them." His eyes were stretched even wider now, and his voice was little more than a rasping whisper as he said, *"They are to us as we are to apes."*

"What does that mean?" I asked desperately.

Mr. Peterson looked confused, as if I was missing some

obvious point and he wasn't sure how to explain it in easier terms.

"It means that . . . we are the only . . . the only ones left . . . four . . . four against all . . ."

His voice trailed off and suddenly his face lost its urgent intensity, going slack, almost sleepy.

"I don't understand," I said. "Tell me what you mean."

Tears streamed from down his face and he gave me the weakest of smiles.

"I . . . I . . . I've *groken ny gicycle*," he said in Mr. Peebles's voice, a falsetto sound of utter insanity. "I *get* you don't really care *ooh-at's* wrong with ne."

And then he started laughing, laughing in that awful, high-pitched way that he reserved for his ugly-headed ventriloquist's dummy.

I got up feeling very cold and very scared. We all backed away from that terrible sound and left the green.

CHAPTER 10

Mrs. O'Donnell's house was on Carlyle Road, an old terrace that ran behind the High Street. It's one of those narrow streets, which means people have to park half on and half off the curbs.

We were midway up the road when Mrs. O'Donnell stopped. A beautifully clipped hedge bordered a tiny concrete garden and I thought we had arrived at her house, but she pointed through an open front door where two young children—a boy and a girl—had been in the process of coming out, perhaps on their way to the green, before being struck down by the . . . *event*.

The girl was waiting by the front door; the boy was stuck, mid-stride, in the hallway.

"Annie and Nicholas Cross," Mrs. O'Donnell said, and I thought I could see tears in her eyes. "I babysit for them now and then. She's six and he's eight. They're nice kids. What could have done this to them? To everyone?"

I wondered why she was asking us.

But what *could* have done it?

And then I made one of those unlikely connections the human brain is so good at making—joined together a couple of pieces of information that really didn't belong together.

Today's events and something that happened a couple of years ago.

There were some local kids near Naylor's farm on the outer reaches of the village, who swore blind that they saw lights in the sky over one of old man Naylor's grain silos. Bright, moving lights that didn't behave like ordinary aircraft.

To start with, there was a certain amount of sneering and laughing, but they were absolutely certain, and a report made it to the local weekly paper.

Although why alien craft always appear over grain silos and open fields rather than over towns and cities has always bothered me. If there really were aliens flying their spaceships above places in the middle of nowhere . . . well, maybe they aren't all that smart, you know?

Anyway, I suddenly started wondering whether it might be connected. I'd joked about UFOs earlier to Lilly—went down like a lead battleship too—but what other alternatives were there?

A chemical accident.

A biological plague.

A fracture in the fabric of time.

Were they any more likely?

I thought about the mad things that Mr. Peterson had said. Things I had ignored because . . . well, because they *were* so mad. But had he seen something that our eyes hadn't?

Had we been *invaded* and didn't even know it?

I shook my head to clear the stupid thought. What kind of alien invasion would cause people to stand still, for goodness' sake? I mean, how was that an invasion exactly?

I was filling the gaps in with what I knew, and painting them ET green.

Surely that was a sign of madness too.

Mrs. O'Donnell's house was tidy and neat, just like the woman herself. Actually, being honest about my first impression, it was *way* more than tidy: as if its contents had just come out of protective coverings. There was a heavy smell of furniture polish and artificial flowers. I guessed she spent a lot of her free time cleaning.

The walls were pastel pink with paintings of flowers and horses hanging on them. The books that graced her neat shelves were all of the chick-lit variety. I realized that Mrs. O'Donnell had, at no point, expressed concern for a *Mr.* O'Donnell, and her house reflected his absence from her thoughts.

The TV was small and old school, and it wasn't even hooked

up to a hi-fi. There was a DVD player and a cheap Freeview box. She switched on the TV and its screen came up blank. No static, just a blue screen. She flicked through the channels slowly with a remote, as if she wasn't 100 percent certain how it worked. There were no stations, just the same neutral blue screen. She killed the TV and shook her head.

The living room led on through an arch into a dining area, with the corner made into a workstation. A very neat workstation: computer, keyboard, mouse. No piles of papers or stacks of disks.

She pushed the POWER button to boot up her iMac and we waited for it to warm up.

It only took a few seconds of absolute silence for us to realize that something had gone wrong.

The usual Apple loading screen did not appear.

In its place were strings of characters that did not belong in any alphabet I have ever seen. Odd, hook-shaped characters; spiky circles that flexed and pulsed; characters that twisted together, seeming to revolve on the screen; characters that looked like they could be meant to represent human eyes; and a large number of short lines that bent at such weird angles they made me feel . . . *uncomfortable* viewing them.

It was like a language, I guess, but with letters that moved, constantly changing, evolving.

"What is this . . . ?" Mrs. O'Donnell asked, desperately pushing keys.

"It looks like a virus," Lilly said, staring over Mrs. O'Donnell's shoulder.

"I don't think it's a virus," I said. "Look at the way it's set out. It looks like a document. I think that it's text, just not in a language we can read."

Lilly made a *hmph* sound.

"What?" I asked her, perplexed.

"You are *such* an idiot," she said.

"What did I do?" I protested.

"I think that it's text, just not in a language we can read," she mimicked me with a cruel tone that made it sound a whole lot sillier than when I'd said it. "What's that even supposed to mean? And how is it supposed to help us?"

I suppose that it's time to throw some light on this . . . oddness . . . that was happening between Lilly and me.

Just to get it out of the way.

Now seems as good a time as any.

You see, I actually went out with Lilly for a few weeks.

This was quite a while before Simon did.

We were a couple of kids at school who fancied each other and ended up being girlfriend and boyfriend.

For a while.

I don't really need to go into all the details. You . . . well, you know how it is. You spend a few break times together, you hold hands, you write her name in an exercise book or two, feel stupidly jealous if you see her talking to any other boy. You laugh at each other's jokes, and find yourself thinking about her when you're not together.

I even went back to her house once.

Just once.

That was kind of the trouble, really.

I was invited round for "tea" one evening.

Lilly's family lives in the old village store. From the road it's pretty unremarkable: a flinted facade of the kind that's common in Millgrove, a couple of bay windows that were probably display windows when the place was a shop, a nondescript front door.

I'd never given it a second look.

It looked like an ordinary house.

When I walked through the front door, trailing behind Lilly, I found myself in a room that was shop-sized. Literally. The whole ground floor of my house would have fit in that one room.

It had a black-beamed ceiling and what looked like an acre of parquet flooring. There was a grand piano in there and it didn't take up much of the available space. There were two vast, but somehow elegant sofas that must have cost thousands of pounds; there were oil paintings of horses and hounds on the walls that were . . . well, real paintings, not prints.

I'd never seen anything like it. Not in real life. And I realized two things:

1. Lilly's parents were far wealthier than she had ever let on, and
2. I could never invite her back to my house.

I pictured showing Lilly into the front room of my house: a tiny room with no art on the walls; no pianos; a little, old TV; and a tatty, three-piece suit.

I imagined how bad, how ashamed that would make me feel.

And then I met her parents.

Lilly's mother prepared the food on a huge, enameled Aga. We sat on wooden pews around an ancient table, and Lilly's parents made conversation that was bright, witty, and very, very clever. They talked about music, literature, and art; they made instant jokes and witty asides, and they made me feel so uncultured and stupid that I squirmed in my seat every time they spoke to me.

I pictured taking Lilly back to meet my folks.

Discussions about rubbish television.

Chris and his endless chatter about football.

I felt ashamed at the very thought of it.

I started avoiding her soon after.

I invented phony reasons and engineered even phonier arguments.

I stood her up. Twice.

Time passed, she got the message, and she broke up with me.

Then, while I was playing at being Dad, I neglected Simon. I was too busy. Or thought I was. And in that time he and Lilly became friends.

Then more than friends.

And I hated my parents for not being like Lilly's parents.

I hated my mum for not having an Aga.

I hated my dad for leaving us.

I hated them both for letting my best friend get the girl I had been too embarrassed to have for myself.

I never told Lilly why I acted the way I did. She must have thought I was the world's biggest jerk.

At least she hadn't seen the truth.

Now, next to her at Mrs. O'Donnell's house, I realized that sniping at me was partly her way of dealing with things. Just as mine was making jokes and Mr. Peterson's was to cut himself off from it all, to deny its existence.

If her comments also meant she was paying me back for being such an idiot to her, then I reckoned I deserved it.

"I'm only saying that the groupings of symbols could be words," I said calmly. "Maybe we just don't understand the language they're written in."

There was a moment of silence and, in the space between sounds I thought I heard something. Something outside and probably distant, but as I listened harder, it seemed to be getting closer.

It was a weird, disquieting sound, a bit like distant thunder, but somehow more *electrical* sounding.

Synthetic thunder?

What was I thinking?

"It makes no difference," Mrs. O'Donnell said bleakly. If she had heard the sound, she didn't show it. "The television can't pick up a signal. The computer displays these weird symbols. The phones are down. So are the radios."

She turned the computer off in disgust and turned around to face us.

"We're on our own for now," she said.

In the silence that followed I realized that the odd sound I had heard had stopped.

Had it just been a symptom of my already overstretched imagination?

Or was there really something out there?

Something that roared like counterfeit thunder?

That was moving towards us, silently now?

I shuddered and looked to Mrs. O'Donnell for some kind of reassurance.

The fear in her eyes told me there was none there to be found.

CHAPTER 11

I guess I have always believed that grown-ups have all the answers.

They behave as if they do.

Looking at Mrs. O'Donnell's face I suddenly realized something: it's not true. Adults are just making things up as they go along. And when they're scared, adults have no more answers than us kids.

Mrs. O'Donnell was scared and she didn't know what to do. Everything that she knew and thought had been—

EDITOR'S NOTE

We have absolutely no way of knowing just how Side Two would have ended if the tape had not run out. Many papers and book chapters have set out to explore this interruption to the story, but they are all just guesses. They are not worth looking at here, because they cloud the issues rather than bring them into focus. When Graysmark argues that "(T)he largest truth of the Straker account lies in the silent spaces between tapes," he allows himself to fall into what Nightingale calls "the fallacy of the gaps." The meaning of the gaps cannot be known, measured, or estimated.

KYLE STRAKER'S SECOND TAPE

. . . my train of thought?

My throat is dry. Dry and scratchy. I think this is the most talking that I have ever done in my life. In one go, that is.

Funny thing is, I don't even know if anyone will ever listen to these tapes. I'm not even sure why I thought it was such a good idea to make them. I just wanted to leave a record, for the four of us, for any more people like us that are left, so that we will not be forgotten.

I think that's what we all want, in the end.

To know that we left footprints when we passed by, however briefly.

We want to be remembered.

So remember us.

Please.

Remember us.

CHAPTER 12

Things never happen the way you think they are going to. Too many random factors between thought and action, I guess. My dad used to sum it up with this weird golf saying: *there's many a slip twixt the cup and the lip.*

NOTE—*"Golf"*

Two things here:

1. Golf was a sport thought to be an early version of what we now call "Flagellum." Golf, however, used an external, manufactured club to strike a "ball" towards a much closer target (hundreds of meters, rather than tens of kilometers) called a "hole," which was traditionally marked by a flag.

2. The proverb "many a slip . . ." is unlikely to have ever originated from the sport of golf, and is more likely to do with the way primitive humans used to drink by raising a drinking vessel (or cup) to the mouth (which used to feature "lips," or movable organs that fringed the mouth and were used

for assisting eating, for rudimentary sensing, and for speech formation). See Bathgate's *Vestiges of Barbarism—What Our Bodies Used to Be.*

We left Mrs. O'Donnell's house in a flat depression. The idea was to go back to Mr. Peterson, check he was okay, then head out of the village on the Crowley Road to see how far the phenomenon stretched.

Easy plan.

We were halfway down the road when Mrs. O'Donnell stopped walking.

"They've gone," she said, and I realized she was at the house where the boy and girl had been standing, frozen in the act of coming out of their house.

Had been.

They weren't there now.

The hallway was empty.

CHAPTER 13

We hit the High Street at a run.

Gone was the heaviness that had settled over our minds and bodies, now we felt light as clouds. If the Cross children were gone, then surely it was likely that *they had moved themselves.* If that was true, maybe everyone else was moving again.

Suddenly, we stopped running. People were moving down the High Street.

People.

Were.

Moving.

In fact, it was a great number of people and they were walking as a crowd, away from the village green and heading for, I guessed, their houses.

People.

Moving.

It was wonderful.

And if they looked a little dazed—staring about themselves as if seeing an unfamiliar place—then that was probably to be expected after what had just happened to them.

I wondered if they realized anything *had* happened at all, or whether they had just been switched back on, with no sense that time had even passed.

Relief flooded through me, as if my world had suddenly been set back onto its proper axis. I saw Lilly's face register her own internal relief. Tension replaced by excitement. And a hint of a smile.

I knew that the smile was for Simon and I felt an eel of jealousy uncurl within my stomach.

NOTE—*"Eel of Jealousy"*

This is quite a bizarre phrase, because an eel was a snakelike fish of the type we now refer to as an Anguilliforme. How this related to jealousy is unknown, although Kenton argues for it being a kind of metaphor for the feeling the primitive emotion caused within the individual. LeGar, however, points to a fragment of a text called "Stargate SG-1," which suggests that a parasitic creature of this type may have been present within certain individuals. It didn't last.

Whatever it was that had occurred was over now.

The people of the village were making their way back home.

I noticed my parents and brother in the crowd, then turned to Mrs. O'Donnell, who offered me a reassuring smile.

I smiled back, nodded at Lilly, and made my way through the crowd to join them.

CHAPTER 14

There was the oddest of moments when my mum's eyes met mine and she seemed to look straight through me, as if she didn't recognize me, or was looking past me, in search of . . .

In search of what?

I couldn't even finish the thought because suddenly her eyes flicked back to me. They *saw* me as if I had just materialized out of thin air. They locked on me then, and I saw recognition flood into her eyes. Her mouth turned up into a smile.

"Kyle," she said, and there was a softness to her voice that hadn't been there for a while. The way she said my name *before* Dad went and broke her heart.

I ran to her and she hugged me tight.

"I was so scared," I told her.

"Scared, poppet?" she comforted me. "Now what on earth is there to be scared about?"

Dad squeezed my arm.

"There's nothing to be scared about," he whispered, and again it was a voice from the past. "We're here."

I was crying then, with hot, fat tears rolling down my cheeks. I didn't care how it looked, or whether people I went to school with were watching.

"I thought I'd lost you," I said.

"We're here," Mum soothed. "And we're not going anywhere."

"What's all this about?" Dad asked, and his voice was concerned and open, instead of defensive.

We made our way back home as part of the crowd, with the sun shining down upon us. I felt exhausted, utterly frazzled.

Mum and I sat down in the front room as Dad rattled about in the kitchen making cups of tea.

Then we sat there, my parents' faces looking full of concern and compassion.

Dad reached over and grabbed hold of Mum's hand, something he hadn't done since he came back to us—at least not without Mum bristling like a terrified cat.

We sipped tea, and the madness faded away.

"You were shaking when we found you," Mum said. "I haven't seen you so frightened since your father told you about the bogeyman and you thought he was under your bed."

"He *was* under my bed," I said, and smiled.

Dad laughed.

"So what did happen?" he asked.

"You wouldn't believe me if I told you."

"Try us."

For a moment I didn't want to tell them, I didn't want to think about what had happened, what it all meant. It was all right now.

But I *had* to tell them.

I had to at least *try* to get some kind of explanation for the weirdness.

Would they think I was mad? If they did, I had witnesses to prove what I was saying.

So I took a deep breath and started speaking.

It all poured out in a mad gush, interrupted only by sobs and chokes.

The whole story.

My parents listened, almost without comment, occasionally asking questions when I wasn't clear enough, or the story got a little confused in my head.

When I was done, Dad looked puzzled.

"Well, Kyle," he said. "That's just not the way we remember it." His voice had an odd edge to it, as if there was something sharp and hard beneath the surface.

I noticed he was still holding Mum's hand as he spoke.

He smiled.

"We watched you go up onstage," he said. "We saw Danny hypnotize you." His smile deepened as if at a private joke. "Actually, he made you pretend that you were a man with no control over his limbs, trying to direct traffic in the

81

center of rush-hour London—and yes, before you ask, we laughed a lot."

Mum and Dad exchanged a smile at the memory and my cheeks felt hot. I must have looked like a total idiot. In all honesty it was probably as embarrassing as my stand-up act. I had a memory flash of Dad with his phone camera and hoped he wasn't about to get out photographic proof of my unconscious humiliation.

Instead he went on.

"Danny made Lilly Dartington think she was walking a tightrope over Niagara Falls. He made our postman think he was called Mr. Peebles, and that he had a dummy called Rodney Peterson. He ended up doing his ventriloquism act again, but in reverse. And Kate, the woman from Happy Shopper, he had her auditioning for the Sydney Opera, but realizing she was naked halfway through her first aria."

Dad laughed.

"He's very good," he said. "Danny, I mean."

"But what happened *after*?" I asked him.

There was a blank look from my parents, which was kind of similar to the look my mum had given me when I met her on the High Street. A kind of look at me that seemed focused on something in the distance past me.

"Nothing," they said together.

In unison.

The word came from each of them at precisely the same time, with the same kind of intonation.

"Nothing happened," Dad said as if reading from a cue card.

"Nothing at all," Mum said as if reading from another cue card.

"Danny woke you all up," Dad said. "And we all went home."

They were acting very . . . *weird*, like they were slightly . . . I don't know . . . *out of sync* with the world.

Or with *my* world.

If that makes sense.

Something had changed, but I couldn't work out what. They looked like my parents, sounded like them, but something about them was off. I was getting a peculiar vibe off them.

And they hadn't noticed the odd thing that Dad had just said.

Danny woke you all up. And we all went home.

I left it at that. My head hurt from all the input. I was coming down off adrenaline and had a sick feeling in my stomach that just wouldn't go away. As if it was the air I was breathing that had somehow turned sour and was making me ill.

I gabbled out something about feeling tired and needing to lie down.

My parents nodded and agreed.

I went to my room to think.

CHAPTER 15

My room was small and poky and wasn't tidy.

Ever.

And quite often it smelled of socks.

There were posters on the walls, a couple advertising films—*Serenity* and *Blade Runner*—a couple promoting bands—*Pendulum* and *Kings of Leon*—and then a storage system that used the floor more than it did the cupboards. My mum was always on at me to clean it and I usually argued that my room was just too small for me to keep all my stuff in *and* keep it tidy.

I ignored the mess.

I looked at my watch and saw that everything that had happened—from Danny calling up us up onstage, right through to the present moment—had all fit into just a little bit over an hour.

I didn't believe it.

But my bedside clock confirmed it.

Time is such a weird thing. A physics teacher once tried to tell me that time is relative, not constant, but I still have no idea what that means in practical terms. I mean, I tried to find out, but only managed to read about ten paragraphs of *A Brief History of Time* before my eyes started to bleed. I *do* know that boring hours last forever, and excitement makes time run like a film on fast-forward.

It had been a fast-forward kind of day.

Lying on my bed, hands behind my head, I tried to think it all through.

However much my parents might say otherwise, something had happened.

But what?

What had happened to the four of us who were hypnotized?

And what had happened to the rest of the people who weren't?

The last question was the one that my mind was obsessing over. It lay there behind my eyes, a trapdoor spider of a thought taking bites out of the relief I'd felt when everyone started moving again.

NOTE—*"Trapdoor Spider"*

Kyle seems to like the notion that his thoughts and feelings are akin to parasitic creatures inhabiting his body. The use of the "trapdoor spider" here seems to back up my belief that the "eels" from earlier were purely figurative. Unless, of course, LeGar uncovers another partial text that suggests that spiders in heads have historical precedent.

What had happened to *them*?

Mr. Peterson thought he saw something, and it had made him curl up on the stage in utter terror. He had said that *They are to us as we are to apes*—whatever that was supposed to mean—and he had been pointing to the people sitting, frozen all that time. He believed that something had happened to *them*, not to *us*.

He said that we were the last four left.

But what did that mean?

Did it mean anything at all?

I thought maybe it did.

Mum and Dad were getting on with each other. Not just getting on, though, they were behaving as if the cold war of the last few months hadn't happened at all.

So what had happened to bring them together so suddenly?

So *unnaturally*?

What had changed?

What *could* have changed?

It wasn't as if watching me behave like a hypnotized numpty was going to make them forget their differences.

And then there was that odd thing that Dad had let slip when I told him what had happened. First had been that dismissive *Well, Kyle, that's just not the way we remember it*, and then that confusing account of the end of the talent show.

Danny woke you all up, Dad had said, *and we all went home*.

It didn't fit.

Danny had been the sixth act.

There had been a whole lot more acts to come *after* Danny.

Danny woke you all up, and we all went home.

I could imagine some of the horrors that would have come after Danny: lame karaoke, awful dance routines, someone playing the recorder, a kid with a new electric guitar who thought he was the next Jimi Hendrix.

Danny woke you all up, and we all went home.

Then there was the inevitable prize giving that always took half an hour longer than it needed to.

Then a repeat of the winning act.

Polite applause.

The end.

Danny woke you all up, and we all went home.

The contest had been, at best, a quarter of the way to being over.

There was a whole lot more to enjoy.

Or endure.

They didn't even stop to announce a winner.

Danny woke you all up, and we all went home.

Liar, I thought.

What had really happened?

Mr. Peterson had said, *It means that . . . we are the only . . . the only ones left . . . four . . . four against all . . .*

I realized then that this wasn't over yet. It wasn't *happy-ever-after*. And it certainly wasn't *everything back to normal.*

This, I realized, was just the beginning.

But the beginning of what?

CHAPTER 16

I wasn't going to get any answers from my parents, that much seemed certain. They either didn't know what had happened, or weren't saying.

The first explanation was scary because our parents are always supposed to have the answers to our questions.

The second explanation was worse still.

That they knew *exactly* what had happened and were keeping it from me.

But what reason could they have for lying to me?

The questions kept circling around in my head, and I would have given anything for them to stop. But they wouldn't.

What had really happened to us all?

I couldn't sort this out on my own.

I tried the TV I've got in my room, which meant hunting for the remote control in the chaos that covered the floor.

I turned over books and comics, clothes and papers, finally finding it hiding under my pillow.

I stabbed the ON button with my thumb and the TV was all white.

Still no way of seeing what was going on in the rest of the world.

I found myself wishing that my parents had bought me the laptop I'd been asking for. The one I'll get when my school-work improves, or when I stop daydreaming, or when I start keeping my room tidy.

The only computer in the house was my dad's, in his study, but I didn't trust my parents and was pretty sure he wouldn't want me using it.

So who could I trust?

There were only three names on my list: the three people who had been with me when the rest of the village played musical statues.

Top of that list was Lilly.

Sure, she hated me because I dumped her and never gave her a reason.

But. But. But.

Why should that get in the way?

She'd never know how much it hurt to let her out of my life, or how much I've regretted it every time I've seen her and Simon together.

We'd been through the same events.

I needed to speak to her.

I sat up.

If I saw Lilly, then Simon would most likely be there, and maybe I could see if he was acting oddly too.

I could find out what he remembered about the talent show, and see if it matched my parents' memory or mine.

I'd made up my mind.

I was going to get to the bottom of this.

I got downstairs to find Dad standing in the hall, seemingly studying the wallpaper.

And, more important, he was blocking the front door.

He made a show of pretending he wasn't waiting for me, but had no other reason for standing where he was. He turned when he heard me on the stairs and his face lit up as if he was pleased to see me. Didn't make it to his eyes, though. They looked at me coldly.

"Ah, Kyle," he said. "Are you feeling better?"

I nodded.

"I'm fine," I told him. "Lying down seems to have cleared my head a bit."

"Good." Dad nodded, perhaps to demonstrate that this was indeed good. "There's someone here to see you."

I hadn't heard anyone arrive, but then I sort of had been lost in my own thoughts.

So who was it?

Lilly? That had to be who it was. She probably had a whole bunch of questions that needed answers too. Well, she'd beaten me to it.

Dad opened the living room door and ushered me inside.

Mum was sitting in her chair, the one with the various remote controls in pouches on the arm, while the other chair was occupied by our local GP, Dr. Campbell.

The last time I'd seen him had been months ago, when I'd injured my wrist playing tennis with Simon.

Dad followed me in and pointedly shut the living room door behind him.

"Hello, Kyle," the doctor said, his old face watchful.

"Hi," I said, my mind racing.

I sat down on one end of the sofa, while Dad took up a place at the other end, leaving plenty of distance between us. The three adults looked dreadfully serious, and if I didn't know better I'd have thought I was in a great deal of trouble for something I had done.

Dr. Campbell smiled at me, but it was a controlled smile. He smoothed out some wrinkles from his trouser leg.

"Your parents asked me over," he said. "They thought that you might be feeling . . . ill."

I smiled back.

"Me?" I said. "I'm fine."

"Good. Good." The doctor nodded. "So you don't feel feverish? Or disoriented?"

"No, I really am fine."

"Your parents are quite worried about you." His eyes narrowed to slits and it looked like he was watching for my reactions to his words. "That was quite a story you told them earlier, wasn't it?"

I didn't like this.

I didn't like it at all.

My mouth was dry and I felt panicked. I didn't answer. I just sat there looking at the doctor, wondering where this was going.

Dr. Campbell sighed.

"Tell me what happened today," he said, and his voice had a coaxing tone to it.

"I don't know," I said. "I mean, I'm really not sure."

"But your parents told me what you told them, that everyone in the village turned to statues for . . . how long did you say?"

He raised an overly furry eyebrow at me.

I shook my head.

"I didn't." My throat felt scratchy.

He was scrutinizing me as if I were a germ under his microscope.

"You didn't say? Or you didn't really experience it?"

I nodded. Evasive.

The doctor frowned, turned to my dad, and said, "I'm getting nowhere. Perhaps you could try . . . ?"

Dad tried to give me a reassuring smile.

"C'mon, Kyle," he urged. "Just tell the doctor what you told us. Maybe he can help."

For some odd reason I got the impression that helping me wasn't very high on Doc Campbell's list of goals here. So I made a deliberate show of massaging my temples and squeezing my eyes shut, as if I was desperately trying to remember something. It wasn't an Oscar-worthy performance, but it wasn't half bad.

"I . . . I can't remember," I said after a few moments. "I think I nodded off upstairs and it's all just slipping away."

The doctor shrugged.

"I suspect that you have had some kind of reaction to the hypnosis," he said gravely. "A dream, if you like, while in a highly suggestible state. Your mind has invented an alternative version of reality where it was *everyone else* who got hypnotized, while you and other volunteers were the only ones that were really awake. It's a kind of inverted version of the way things really were."

He brushed at his trouser leg again, his eyes never leaving mine.

"You need to sleep," he said. "It will give your mind time to sort itself out, allow it to put fantasy and reality back in their proper places."

He smiled widely.

"Doctor's orders," he said.

"I *do* feel very tired," I lied.

"Then that's settled," the doctor said brightly. "You rest. Stay in bed the rest of the day. I'll stop by tomorrow to make sure that everything is okay. I'll leave a couple of pills with your parents in case you find sleep difficult."

"Thank you, Dr. Campbell."

"It's what I'm here for," he said.

No, it's not, I thought instinctively.

I had to get away from here. To find Lilly. Maybe Mrs. O'Donnell. Talk to them about what they remembered, and find out their impressions of the village now the event was "over."

Then I needed to find Rodney Peterson and find out exactly what he thought he saw.

"I think I'll go and lie down a bit more," I said.

"Good boy," Dr. Campbell said. "You'll soon see that it was all just a horrible nightmare."

Liar, liar, I thought. *I know it. You know it.*

I had a sudden flash of intuition and decided I'd play a hunch.

"I'm glad Mum and Dad called you," I said.

"So am I, young man," he said.

"Lucky you were by the phone on a Saturday too."

"I'm always on call," he explained. "I guess it's the curse of being the only doctor in the village."

I got up and crossed the room towards the door. The

telephone was on its cradle on a table nearby. I feinted for the door, went for the phone instead, picked it up, and switched it on.

I got a dial tone.

Dr. Campbell was on his feet, starting towards me, but not before I punched in those three numbers.

999.

The doctor reached me and tried to get the phone from me, but I held him off for the few seconds I needed. When he finally wrenched the phone from my hand, I had already confirmed what I had suspected: there was nothing and nobody on the line.

Just those clicks and hisses I knew would be there.

"I'll be in my room," I said quietly, and made my way up the stairs.

CHAPTER 17

My experiment had proved that Dr. Campbell had lied—Mum and Dad couldn't have called him: the phone wasn't working—but past that I couldn't go.

I needed to get out of the house.

The question now was: *how*?

I'd talked myself up into my room, where I was now a virtual prisoner.

There was the doctor who was here to "check on me." And there was Dad blocking the door when I went downstairs.

This was all madness. An ordinary life turned upside down in the space of a few short hours.

I was going to have to improvise.

I sat down on my bed.

The sunlight coming through the window made my eyes hurt.

I stood up, went over to the window, and opened it. My bedroom occupied the space directly over dad's study, with a view of a small front garden that nature was busy taking back from my parents.

My parents and Dr. Campbell were talking in the living room, which we called the front room even though, technically speaking, it looked out across the back garden. If they stayed there for a few more minutes, and if I was brave—or foolish—enough to climb out of my window, there was a chance I could be well away from the house before they even realized I was gone.

I sized up the drop.

It was somewhere between four and six meters, I reckoned.

Risk assessment: a broken leg at least, probably worse.

But if I lowered myself down, so that I was hanging from the window frame with my arms fully extended, it would cut about two meters from the drop.

Risk assessment: still a possible broken leg, more likely a twisted or sprained ankle.

The problem with both of these courses of action was that I needed to be certain that I could still walk when I reached the ground.

The risk was too high.

Off to the right side of my window, touching the side of the house, was an old tree. In high winds the branches would often tap against the panes of glass in my window.

It was a good meter away from me. I could, however, jump across and then climb down the tree.

A meter jump.

The simplest of leaps.

If I was on the ground.

But I wasn't on the ground, was I?

I was four to six meters up and if I missed the tree, or missed getting a good grip, or got a good grip on a branch that decided to give way, I would fall the whole distance.

And get the "worse" from the first risk assessment: broken legs, possible broken back, with the added chance of cuts, grazes, and bruises.

A one-meter jump.

I took out one of the cans of Red Bull from my jacket pocket, opened it, downed it in one, and then clambered out through the window.

I put my feet on the narrow, sloping ledge, had my bottom sitting on the frame.

The window opened to the right and was blocking any jump.

I took a deep breath and stood up, feet braced on the ledge, arms using the window frame to pull myself up and through. Holding on to the left side of the frame with my left hand, I used my right to grab the concrete base of the guttering that passed overhead and I turned my body 180 degrees, so I was facing back towards the house.

I used my left hand to close the window behind me.

I reckoned that I had just passed the point of no return.

Another deep breath, and I shuffled, bit by bit, to the ledge closest to the tree.

One meter. Easy on the ground.

The tree was an aging beech with rust-colored leaves. It had branches pointing upwards from a thick, gnarled trunk that someone, many years ago, had stopped from growing too high by sawing it off about three meters from the ground. It made a platform for me to aim at, if I could make it through the screen of branches that surrounded it.

One meter.

I held on to the gutter concrete with my right hand and shuffled my feet around so I was facing the middle of the tree, swallowed a ball of spit that felt about the size of a clementine, gritted my teeth, bent my knees, and then jumped.

CHAPTER 18

My legs threw me forwards, and suddenly I was rootless, at the mercy of scientific forces like mass and velocity, resistance and gravity. It was terrifying and exhilarating. I threw myself at the tree and opened my arms to catch it.

I hit a tall, upright branch full face, crashing into it, hard. It made me dizzy—the pain I ignored for now—and I felt myself starting to fall.

I thrashed my arms and clawed for purchases, feeling the hardness of the wood slipping from my grasp. Leaves and smaller branches whipped at my face as I started to tumble downwards. The moment stretched out in perfect slow motion.

I'm dead, I thought calmly, far more calmly than I would have expected under the circumstances.

I think it was that calmness that saved my life.

It allowed me to give survival one more go.

I made a last, deliberate grab for a branch and it felt as if my arms were being torn from their sockets. My head was thrown backwards, and my back arched at a painful angle. Twigs slapped my face and I could taste leaves in my mouth.

But I held on, sweating and trembling, hugging the branch to my chest. My legs fought for even safer purchase and found it.

A few breaths to calm myself, and to get my heart beating at a more normal rate, then I inched myself down the branch, towards the trunk. Evolution was all well and good, but a monkey would have done a far better job of this than me.

In time, I reached the sawed-off "platform" I had seen from my window and tried to lower myself onto it. The angle that the branch met the platform was difficult, but I adjusted my position on the branch and pretty much slid onto it. It was a small area, but wide enough for me to catch my breath and prepare for the next phase of my descent.

I was crouching there, braced on all sides by branches, when suddenly the front door opened and Dr. Campbell stepped out onto the path, off to my left and only a short distance below me. I felt certain that he would see me, but there was no way to conceal myself further, so I waited with a leaden feeling in my stomach.

Dr. Campbell was speaking to one or both of my parents, who remained inside the house. His voice was loud enough for me to hear everything.

"Make sure he stays where he is," he said grimly. "I'm sorry, but it is clear that he is one of the zero-point-four. There is nothing that can be done for him. He will have to be dealt with."

My mother uttered a strange, strangled sound.

"I will return soon," the doctor said, ignoring her. "Drug him if you have to."

He turned and walked away from the house and his route brought him even closer to my hiding place. I drew myself up as if making myself fractionally smaller would stop him from spotting me if he decided to look my way.

But he didn't look my way, and I watched him go, heard the front door of my house close. It sounded loud and hollow like the door of a tomb.

I was one of the *0.4.*

That was what Dr. Campbell had said: 0.4.

What on earth did that mean?

I waited a few seconds, slipped through the cover of branches, and shimmied down the trunk of the old beech tree.

I had thought that I was scared before.

He will have to be dealt with, the doctor had said, and a chill had passed down my spine.

Did it mean that I was going to be killed? It had certainly sounded that way to me.

There is nothing that can be done for him.

He is one of the zero-point-four. Drug him if you have to.

What in the hell was going on?

I set off for Lilly's house to find out.

I had to know if what I was . . .

. . . yeah, I know. I'm just in the middle of . . . I will . . . I just need to . . .

[silence]

CHAPTER 19

I felt like a criminal on the run, making my way through enemy territory. I was terrified of bumping into anyone, but there was no one around *to* bump into. The village, it seemed, was deserted. Like Mum and Dad, everyone had to be back at home.

Awaiting further instructions.

I couldn't trust anyone.

Dr. Campbell had said that I was one of the *0.4,* and that I would *have to be dealt with*. Did that make everyone else in the village, everyone I knew, part of the other group?

Zero-point-four—that was four-tenths. Four over ten. Two-fifths. Was that how few people like me still existed? Had the other 0.6 been *changed* somehow?

0.6.

Six-tenths.

More than half.

Was I now in the minority?

And how mad did *that* sound?

I didn't know, not for certain, that there was anything going on here at all.

I was running scared through the village because . . . because of *what*?

Okay, something had happened in Millgrove; something that had affected everyone in the village except for four people who were hypnotized at the time.

Okay, there was no one on the streets of the village, even though it was a Saturday afternoon and there were *always* people on the streets.

Okay, my parents were acting oddly.

And, okay, the doctor had said a few things that had *sounded* sinister to me.

But maybe Dr. Campbell was right. Maybe I was suffering the aftereffects of hypnosis, and had experienced an inverted version of reality that had meant I had seen everyone else standing still when it was really me who was paralyzed.

Maybe the whole thing was just a fantasy.

Maybe none of it was real.

Maybe it was paranoia and nothing else.

Maybe, maybe, maybe, maybe.

A nightmare, the doctor had called it: Could it be nothing more than that? Could my mind be playing tricks on me?

And that made me think of Jerry Possett. Local guy.

Old—in his seventies, I guess. Probably harmless, but something has gone wrong with his brain. He holds conversations with people who aren't really there, often arguing with these imaginary people in an angry voice.

To Jerry, those people are really there. He sees them, hears them. But they don't exist. And Jerry doesn't seem to know that they don't exist.

The point I'm making here is that our brains play tricks. They can make us see patterns where there are no patterns, see faces in the grain of a wardrobe, castles in cloud formations, something psychologically revealing in an inkblot, can even make ordinarily sane people see UFOs over old man Naylor's grain silos.

I don't know enough about the way the brain works. In fact, I don't have a clue how the brain works. Hundreds of thoughts flow through my brain from one hour to the next and not one of them is about how I'm thinking them.

So what if this was just my brain going off the rails?

Hallucinations.

Paranoia.

A mental breakdown caused by Danny's act.

Meningitis.

Swine flu.

Marsh gas.

Maybe my brain just never wired up all that well to begin with and my whole life had been leading up to this moment, where the bad wiring sends sparks of insanity through my skull and makes me into a Jerry Possett, a nutcase to be avoided.

Maybe *0.4* was simply doctors' jargon for *he's blown a fuse in his brain and we need to get him somewhere secure before he harms himself or others.*

How was it even possible to know if your brain was malfunctioning, because the very thing you need to think it all through is the very thing that might be breaking down in the first place?

Was that some kind of paradox?

Was I mad?

I arrived at Lilly's house and didn't know what to do.

If *her* family was behaving anything like *my* family, they wouldn't let her out; they would be finding excuses to stand by the door and make sure she stayed where she was.

Should I throw stones at her window to attract her attention?

That would be a whole lot easier if I knew which one was her room.

Did I really want to speak to her, anyway?

Did I want to discover that she had no memory of the things I remembered happening to us? Did I really want to find out that all this was happening because my mind was messed up?

I stood there, trying to find a path through it all.

And then the front door of Lilly's house burst open and Lilly came hurtling out towards me.

CHAPTER 20

Lilly saw me standing there and her face registered both surprise and relief. She sprinted towards me and shouted, *"RUN!"* with such urgency that I did just that.

Turned around and ran.

Gave into a stampede instinct inherited from an earlier model of humanity, when saber-toothed tigers stalked the landscape.

I ran, hearing Lilly's feet slapping the pavement just behind me, and it was as if all the tension of the day had suddenly been given an outlet in one mad burst of energy. I drove my legs as fast as they would carry me, away from Lilly's house, without an idea in my head as to why we were running.

Nor where we were running to—it didn't matter.

In those moments, with every thought, breath, and muscle focused on the physical act of running, I felt . . . *free*.

Someone shouted Lilly's name from behind us, and Lilly's footsteps sped up as a result. She gained ground on me, and then she was running next to me.

"Where are we going?" I shouted, feeling the words ripped from my lungs.

"I don't know," she shouted back. "I've just got to get away from . . . from *them*."

I should have been terrified by her words, but instead they actually made me smile. If Lilly was feeling the same way, and her parents had suddenly turned weird, then I wasn't crazy.

My mind was not broken.

I could get through this.

We could get through this.

I think I only realized where we were heading when I started recognizing details of the route from earlier. Some kind of instinct had nudged us towards a place we both thought could give us sanctuary from the madness that was hemming us in on all sides.

We stopped running as we passed the Cross house.

My lungs were burning and there was a fierce pain in my side. Bent over double, I gasped and wheezed and Lilly joined me, even placing a hand on my back.

"Thank you for coming to get me," she said.

"It's okay," I said. "Thanks for the exercise."

She half smiled.

"I'm sorry I got into that silly stuff earlier," she said quietly. "You know, the Simon stuff?"

"It's okay," I said, finally unbending myself and standing up straight. "How is Simon?"

Lilly shook her head. "He's gone," she told me. "Just like all of them. I mean they're there and everything, but they're not. Not really."

She stood up too.

"I must sound crazy," she said.

"Not at all," I said. "I know *exactly* what you mean. They *have* changed."

We carried on towards Mrs. O'Donnell's house.

"Has Dr. Campbell been round for a visit yet?" I asked her.

She nodded. "You too, huh? He told me that I had experienced a powerful hallucination, that it was all a dream I was having, but, like, awake. You?"

"Same story." We were at Mrs. O'Donnell's door now. "I overheard him telling my parents that I was one of the zero-point-four."

Lilly looked at me oddly.

"What's that supposed to mean?" she asked.

I shrugged.

"I haven't got a clue," I said. "I was hoping you'd have an idea."

I lifted my knuckles to the front door, was just about to knock, and turned to Lilly.

"But I think you're one of them too," I said.

Ø Ø Ø

I knocked.

There were noises from within and we stood and waited for them to get closer. Mrs. O'Donnell, it appeared, was in no hurry to open her door. Lilly and I stood there, feeling horribly exposed, and I started thinking that any second two angry sets of parents were going to come around the corner.

Along with Dr. Campbell, no doubt.

Finally, Mrs. O'Donnell opened the door. She raised an eyebrow when she saw us, but ushered us inside without a word. She looked around before closing the front door, as if checking no one was following us.

"I wondered if you might come here," she said, showing us through into the living room.

She was watching us oddly. There was a kind of resigned look, but it was mixed in with what might have been a little sternness at us invading her home again.

"Sorry to disturb—" I began, but the sudden seriousness on her face shut me up.

"Can either of you tell me what the hell is going on?" she demanded.

Lilly and I just shook our heads.

"Nothing good," Lilly said. "My . . . My parents aren't my parents anymore."

"Mine neither," I said.

Mrs. O'Donnell looked at us with a kind of weary acceptance.

"Sit down," she said. "You're both out of breath."

"We ran here," Lilly explained.

We sat down on one of the two sofas. Mrs. O'Donnell disappeared for a few moments and returned with a couple of glasses of orange squash. She handed them out and took a seat on the other sofa.

She asked me what had happened, so I sketched out the events since we had parted on the High Street. All of that seemed an awfully long time ago, even though my watch told me it was just less than an hour. Again my body and my watch disagreed. Time passed weirdly through the looking glass.

Mrs. O'Donnell heard me out, then shook her head and gave an exasperated tut.

"And this thing he called you . . . *zero-point-four* . . . you're sure that's what he said?"

I nodded.

"Well, what do you think *that's* supposed to mean?" she asked.

I told her that I didn't have a clue.

"Zero-point-four," she mused. "Decimals. Pretty meaningless unless you know what they're referring to."

She turned to Lilly, and her face softened a little.

"And what's been happening to you, my dear?"

Lilly sighed.

"It hasn't gone a lot different from Kyle's afternoon," she said. "Simon was, like, *totally* weird. I met up with him when everyone got moving again, and I thought he might be a little . . . I don't know . . . disoriented by the . . . well, you know, whatever it is we're calling all of this."

She waved a hand in the air as if showing how hard this whole thing was to describe.

"Anyway, I started asking him about what had happened to him, you know, all the freezy stuff, and he looked at me like I was mad."

She broke off and then she shook her head.

"No," she said sadly. "Except he didn't look at me like that. I think I could maybe have coped with that. This look was something else." She paused as she tried to pin down her thoughts. "He looked at me like I was . . . *dirt*."

I thought about how Dr. Campbell had looked at me.

"Anyway," she continued, "I got angry with him. At first I thought that he just didn't believe me, or something. But it wasn't that. It was like he was . . . looking down on me. As if he knew something that I didn't. So I got cross with him, and he just walked away. Just turned his back on me and walked. He didn't look back."

Her top lip was quivering and she had tears welling in her eyes.

I felt a sudden flare of anger at Simon for doing that to Lilly, and then a stabbing pang of guilt when I realized it actually hadn't been a whole lot different from what I had done to her after visiting her parents' house.

"So I thought: *Fine. Be like that,*" she continued. "And I walked home—the whole thing rolling round and round inside my brain. And I was scared and angry and confused and angry again. And my parents were like, *What's up with you?* and I didn't even know where to start. And they looked like my parents, they sounded like my parents, but there was something . . . *off* about them, so I told them that we'll talk later and I need to go to my room, and that's when Dr. Campbell rings the doorbell."

"Your parents didn't call Dr. Campbell either?" I asked her.

"No," she said, sounding a little baffled by the question. "They didn't have time. I mean, I hadn't even gone upstairs when he turned up, so how *could* they have called him? And then there's the whole telephones-not-working thing."

Mrs. O'Donnell leaned forwards in her seat. "Do you think *Simon* told him to come round and see you?"

Lilly looked genuinely shocked.

"Why would he . . . ?" she started. "I mean . . . he wouldn't . . . would he?"

Mrs. O'Donnell shrugged.

"I guess it all depends on what we're saying happened to these people," she said. "If we're saying they were merely disoriented by the effect of their . . . of the trance, then, no, I don't think your boyfriend would have told Dr. Campbell to come round to see you."

Mrs. O'Donnell leaned back again.

"But I suspect neither of you is altogether satisfied with that as an explanation for the changes in personality that you noticed."

"It wasn't Simon," Lilly said with such certainty that Mrs. O'Donnell raised an eyebrow of surprise. "And they weren't my parents."

"Well," Mrs. O'Donnell said, "that's certainly a big statement to be making, isn't it?"

Lilly nodded. "It's true," she said.

"But it was *us* who were hypnotized," Mrs. O'Donnell said. "It was us who were put into a trance. This could be just some weird altered version of reality caused by Danny's act."

That had been Dr. Campbell's line, and it had a persuasive logic to it.

"But—" Lilly tried to interrupt but was silenced by a curt wave of Mrs. O'Donnell's hand.

"All I'm saying is that we cannot discount the possibility that there are psychological reasons for all that is happening to us. There are only four of us who saw things one way, and everyone else saw things another. Four individuals out of . . . what—a thousand people? A total of *four* saw something that the other nine hundred and ninety-six did not; whose version of the events would you question first? Honestly, it wouldn't be their version."

I had stopped listening.

My mind had just slotted some details together, and I felt a shiver travel the length of my spine.

"Oh," I said. "Oh no."

Mrs. O'Donnell looked over at me. "What is it?" she asked.

Her voice seemed to travel miles to reach me through the sudden rush of panic I felt.

"Oh no. No no no no—" I said. "How many people did you say live in Millgrove?"

"It's about a thousand," she said. "Just under, I think."

"And how many of us were hypnotized, and are seeing things differently from everyone else?"

"Four," she said as if explaining something to a very dull child.

I didn't care.

The numbers were too terrifying.

"So, what are we, you know, as a percentage of the village's population?" I asked, feeling sick, hoping my math was wrong.

"Well, we would be four out of a thousand . . . which would make us . . . let me think . . ." She stopped. "Oh," she said coldly. Her face had lost some of its color. She looked at me. "That's very good, Kyle," she said. "We *are* in trouble, aren't we?"

"Er, what are we talking about here?" Lilly asked, puzzled.

"What percentage of the village population do we represent?" I asked her.

She shook her head. She should have worked it out way sooner than me.

"The answer is zero-point-four," I said. "We are zero-point-four of a percent."

CHAPTER 21

"We have to find Rodney," Mrs. O'Donnell said, and it took me a few seconds to work out who she was talking about. Even though we had been talking about *the four of us*, it seemed crazy that I could have forgotten about the fate of the fourth person.

Mr. Peterson.

Last seen in a fetal ball on the stage at the talent show.

Where we had left him.

"What happened to him?" I asked. "I mean, after everyone started moving again?"

"I don't know," Mrs. O'Donnell said. "I was so relieved, I . . . I kind of forgot about him. I wandered down the High Street, sort of in a daze, but no one was talking. They were just filing past, completely silent. When I spoke to someone they responded, but it was like they would rather not be talking. As if there was something . . . *new* . . . going on in their heads. They no longer seemed to need to chatter away about nothing. It was eerie. Like . . . like a *funeral*, or something."

I drained the orange squash and rolled the glass around on my trouser leg.

"I . . . I need to ask something," I said. "And . . . well, there's no sort of easy way to . . . Are we talking *aliens* here, do you think?"

Both Lilly and Mrs. O'Donnell looked at me seriously.

It was Lilly who spoke first.

"There's no such thing as aliens," she said definitively.

"Wow, I had no idea that scientists had actually figured that out," I said. "Last I heard they were still keeping an open mind."

"You know what I mean. No little green men and silver spaceships."

"That's not the only kind of alien life possible," I said. "Has anyone seen *Invasion of the Body Snatchers*?"

Mrs. O'Donnell sighed.

"You do realize that was a *film*?" she said caustically. "Not a documentary. And *Invasion of the Body Snatchers* wasn't *really* about aliens. It was about communism, and the remake was about the changing roles of men and women in modern society."

"I thought they were from outer space," I said grumpily.

"In fact, I remember them saying that the pod things that took over people and changed them *were* aliens."

Mrs. O'Donnell's face told me that she thought I had missed the point that she was making.

"The differences in text and subtext aside," she said, "you're thinking that alien pod creatures arrived in Millgrove during a village talent show, and took over everybody except the handful of people hypnotized by a boy magician?"

"Yeah, well, you put it that way and it sounds kinda stupid," I said. "But pod people was only meant as an example, drawn from a science-fiction movie. We *are* agreed that something weird happened, aren't we? I mean, this isn't everyday Millgrove, is it? People that we know are acting *strangely*. We recognize their faces, but no longer them."

"We have no way of knowing what happened when we were in trances on that stage," Mrs. O'Donnell said, "but surely it's more likely that it's *us* who are at fault, that we're seeing things differently—"

"Have you managed to get any TV or radio signals?" I interrupted. "Managed to reach anyone by phone? Are you getting anything on your computer except those symbols we were looking at earlier?"

The look on her face answered my questions for me.

"Look," I said. "I'm a kid. I know that. But it doesn't mean that I'm incapable of seeing what's going on around me. We are in deep, deep trouble here, and if you want the absolute truth, I really don't know what to do about it. But I do know that hiding my head in the sand is the wrong thing to do."

I was getting frustrated and flustered.

I was even waving my arms in the air.

"I think that's why Lilly and I ran here. To get an adult to help us work out a way to put all this right. To bring our parents back to us. To make things go back to the way they were. We need you, Kate."

It was the first time I'd called her—or even thought of her—by her first name.

"Okay," she said, getting to her feet. "We'll go and find Rodney Peterson and then we'll head out of town. We'll get help. We will find people who can figure this thing out."

"Thank you," I said.

She smiled.

"It's okay, Kyle. Now let's get going."

CHAPTER 22

We got into Kate's car and the plan was simple. Stop off and check on Mr. Peterson, and then get the heck out of Millgrove.

None of us were really surprised when it refused to start. The car didn't make a sound. There was no ignition-straining-against-a-flat-battery sound. Not a spark of life in the engine at all.

So we walked down the deserted streets, aware of just how strange it was that they *were* deserted. We knew that there were people inside those houses, but there were no signs nor sounds of life. It made me think of those ghost towns in Westerns. If a couple of spiky tumbleweeds had blown past, I don't think they would have looked out of place.

No life.

Stillness.

It was as if the buildings were brooding, the village was dreaming, and we were just a solitary thought passing through its mind.

The village green was set up for the talent show, but it was deserted too. It looked strange and unsettling.

The stage was empty, and in front of it was chaos. Things that people had brought along with them—picnic food, blankets to sit on, handbags—had been left behind and lay on the grass.

People don't leave their personal effects lying around like that. They take them when they leave. They cling to their possessions almost like it's a reflex.

Nor do they leave people lying on the stage after they have had some kind of mental breakdown.

But they had left Mr. Peterson.

He was still in the same spot we had last seen him.

He was all alone, curled up in a tight ball of his own fear. I suddenly felt terrible that we hadn't thought to go back for him sooner. But we'd had our reasons for forgetting him, I guess. Like the world suddenly turning strange and terrifying.

What was everybody else's excuse?

We approached Mr. Peterson and I could see his body trembling like a leaf. His lips moved as he formed soundless words. His eyes were squeezed shut.

"Mr. Peterson?" I called.

If he heard me there was no visible sign.

"He's in shock," Kate O'Donnell said.

"Why is he *still* like this?" Lilly asked.

"I think he saw something," I said. "I think he saw what happened."

"But he was hypnotized too."

"Everyone's different. Maybe his trance was just a bit shallower than ours."

Lilly shrugged.

"How do we get him to tell us what he saw?" she said.

"Ask nicely?" I suggested.

"You are *such* a loser," she said, but with a smile.

"I know." I smiled back.

Kate knelt over Mr. Peterson and put her hand gently on his shoulder. Initially he recoiled from her touch, but then his eyes opened and he looked at her face.

"It's you," he said. "You came back."

"Of course I did, Rodney."

She reached down and found his hand, wrapped it up in hers, holding it tight.

"And you're still you," he said.

"Yep," she said. "At least I was last time I looked."

"They . . . they didn't . . . get you."

"Who?" Kate asked him. "Who didn't get me?"

"All of them," Mr. Peterson said, suddenly seeming to come back to reality from the dark place inside his own mind where he had been hiding.

"You saw something," Kate said. "I . . . *We* . . . need to know what it was."

Mr. Peterson looked up at her and there was warmth and compassion in his eyes, but there was also fear.

"Something happened to me," Mr. Peterson was saying. "It was like they say in the Bible, when the scales fall from someone's eyes, when they suddenly see the truth behind the visible. I saw the people in the crowd, all of them, and they had become . . . were becoming . . . *something else.* Something . . . impossible."

"What did you see?" That was from Lilly, and there was an urgency that made Mr. Peterson turn to see us standing there for the first time.

"What did I see?" he said. "I don't know how to describe it. I'm used to the way things look . . . *here* . . . in this world, you know? Everything here follows . . . I don't know . . . *visual rules*, about form, perspective, and color. The things we see on this world . . . well, they look like they belong here."

He fought to make it clearer.

"I've never thought about it before: the way that everything that is *from here* looks like it *belongs here.* That even the most dissimilar things in our world—a puddle and an aircraft carrier; an apple and a wisp of smoke; a chicken and the London Gherkin; a road and an ear of sweet corn—they all conform to these same visual rules.

"I know that now, but only because *they*—the ones who

have been changed—don't. The people here . . . they look different now. As if they . . . they don't obey the visual rules of planet Earth. They have . . . other levels, layers, facets . . . I don't know . . . Description is hard when there's nothing you have ever seen that looks anything like what you're seeing."

"So, try."

"They still look like people. They *are* still people, I think. But, somehow, that's a surface image, and what they are now extends way past the surface. Imagine you had a projector that could project a perfectly clear image onto water, but you could still see the water beneath. That's kind of what I saw, I guess. A projection. A new image superimposed over each of the people of this village.

"Most of it I can't even begin to describe. Colors I don't recognize. Textures that make no sense. Constantly in motion, ever-changing, like shadows playing across them . . . and then there are the symbols—"

"Symbols?" Kate interjected. "What do you mean 'symbols'?"

Mr. Peterson shook his head.

"A language, I guess," he said. "Moving across them, across their surfaces. Almost like hieroglyphics . . . with hooks and curls and spikes and eyes as letters. I . . . I think it is a language, but it doesn't behave like our language. It's not flat and on the page; instead, it twists and spins, revealing new elements of each character . . . each word . . . every time it moves."

NOTE—*"Hieroglyphics"*

An extremely ancient form of writing that Rodderick identifies as originating in Egypt: "Hieroglyphics, although antiquated by Kyle Straker's age, were a rebus-like pictorial language that is similar in structure to our own computer code." Benson notes: "Like a precursor to Zapf Dingbats, hieroglyphics made visual images into a language." He then notes: ". . . if you translate the word 'hieroglyphics' into Zapf you get: hieroglyphics." Just why we would want to do this, Benson offers no explanation. But then he is the man who translated the Bible into WingDings.

Kate looked aghast.

"We've seen it," she said.

"You've seen it? How? Where?"

"On my computer screen. It's all the stupid thing will do . . . display these weird characters."

"Your computer?" Mr. Peterson sat up straight. "But that means . . . it's not just them . . . it's . . . *a program?*"

"A computer program?" Kate said.

She turned to me.

"You said it was some kind of language," she said.

I nodded.

"But it didn't look like any computer code I've ever seen . . . ," she said. "So what does it mean?"

I felt cold.

Pieces started fitting together.

"What is it?" Kate asked, noticing my look.

I fought to put my intuition into words.

"I keep coming back to the idea of an alien invasion. . . ."

Lilly made an exasperated sound that I tried to ignore.

Kate asked, "And exactly how would this be a sign of an invasion?"

"It depends how you interpret the word *invasion*." I said. "Perhaps this is *exactly* the way you would invade another planet. I mean, would an alien race really come down in shiny metal ships and try to take over through military might, knowing that we will fight back?

"Or, suppose the strategy was more subtle: infiltrating the planet with alien copies of humans, like the Body Snatchers. There's a danger that the duplicates will be uncovered before there are enough of them to take over.

"Maybe there is another way, and we're seeing it now."

"But how?" Lilly asked.

"What if this computer program we're seeing *is* the invasion?" I said. "What if it's their spaceships and their ray guns and their infiltration devices, all rolled into one?"

"I'm not following you," Lilly said.

I wasn't sure I was following it myself.

"I'm just trying to put pieces together," I confessed. "It's like I can almost see what's happening here, but I can only catch glimpses of it out of the corner of my mind's eye. There's this vague idea that disappears every time I turn to look at it full on."

Lilly nodded, and it seemed that she was urging me on to think about it more.

"Try," she said.

So I did.

"It was the alien language. Which we could see changing and shifting in front of us. How it was lined up on Kate's computer screen. I said it was like sentences. But maybe because I was seeing them on a computer screen it's got me thinking about computers, and about how computers work. Lines and lines of instructions, a particular form of sentence, computer code. What if we're seeing a programming language?"

"Programming what?" Lilly asked.

"That's where I keep coming up blank," I said.

I realized that Mr. Peterson was paying close attention to my words, and I saw him nodding.

"You got something?" I asked.

Mr. Peterson shrugged.

"I'm a postman," he said, and I thought he had just descended back into madness, but then he went on to explain: "And over the last few years there have been a lot of changes in the kind of things we deliver. There are the obvious changes—a lot more parcels from eBay and Amazon; a great deal less of those envelopes containing holiday snaps now that most photography has gone digital.

"The one that seems sad, though, is that there are a lot fewer handwritten letters. People don't send as many small, personal letters as they used to because they tend to stay in touch electronically. They have e-mail, Facebook, and

Twitter. You don't post a letter now, you click a mouse button and it's delivered instantly."

"Is there a point to this story?" Kate asked impatiently.

"The point is that if you want to get in touch with a single person then you *might* send them a letter. An actual, physical, tangible piece of mail. But if you wanted to get in touch with everyone instantly—"

"You'd do it digitally," Lilly finished.

Mr. Peterson nodded.

"Electronically," he said. "With computers."

"A *digital invasion*?" I mused. "What would that even be?"

Mr. Peterson shrugged.

"I don't know," he said. "But mightn't it look a little like today?"

"Hang on a moment," Kate said with horror. "Are we seriously still talking *aliens* here? I mean, come on, there has to be another, rational explanation."

"I'd love to hear it," Mr. Peterson said.

"I just can't believe that we're suddenly in a world where 'aliens' is the first place we're looking for answers," she said incredulously. "Not 'we're still hypnotized and *all* of this is just imaginary.' Not 'mass hysteria' or 'sunspot activity.' Not a 'virus' or 'something in the water.' You know—the kind of answers that sound like they didn't originate on *Fringe* or *Doctor Who*."

The only one of Kate O'Donnell's explanations that held

any water for me—that we were still in a trance and the whole thing was just a fantasy—was the very one that was impossible to prove or disprove. It was like the old question that the film *The Matrix* was based upon: how can you tell if you're just a brain in a jar, experiencing a sophisticated virtual reality program that is flawless in its execution?

The answer is: you can't. So it actually doesn't make much sense entertaining it. If we woke up and found out the day had just been a weird dream, then that would be great, but we couldn't bank on it.

And we certainly couldn't close our minds to other answers *in the hope* that it was right, because we could . . .

EDITOR'S NOTE

The thought here is never returned to. Kyle must have finished the thought on the blank bit of tape. Ernest Merrivale sees the fact as proof that the tapes are all recorded one after the other, without breaks. He suggests that if there had been any break between each tape, Kyle would have rewound the tape to see what he had last said, and thus would have realized that the blank tape was cutting off his words. The error would never have been repeated.

KYLE STRAKER'S LAST TAPE

. . . *going round and round in my head. My brain was making so much noise, but it was about time I started to put all of those thoughts to some good use.*

I tried to think about everything I had seen since waking from the trance on the stage, to find something that would point the way for us to move forwards.

It was then that I remembered Mrs. Birnie.

Proudly recording Danny's act so that there would be a physical record of his appearance at the talent show.

The video camera.

She had been filming it all . . . So what had the video camera caught?

CHAPTER 23

Aware of the odd glances I was getting from the others, I rushed down onto the village green, hoping that Mrs. Birnie had done what most everyone else had—left behind the thing that she was carrying.

It took a couple of minutes of looking around the area to find it, nestled in a discarded sweater. At first I thought that wishing too hard for the thing had made me imagine the flash of reflected sunlight, then I saw it again and headed straight to it.

It was one of the new type of Canon camcorders, a thin slice of metal that concealed some pretty cool tech specs. It was the kind that no longer even needed a tape, working from memory cards and an internal hard drive.

I held it in the air like I'd just won the FA Cup.

Lilly, Kate, and Mr. Peterson were all staring at me as if I had just lost my mind.

"Mrs. Birnie was filming it!" I shouted. "She was filming the whole thing!"

They just kept staring, and I realized that they weren't looking at me at all.

They were looking *behind me.*

I felt like a pantomime character who had suddenly been warned: *"Behind you!"* as I turned my head and stared back over my shoulder.

Then I just felt sick.

The whole village, it seemed, was moving in an unnaturally neat formation: utterly silent, perfectly organized, and heading down the High Street.

Heading towards the village green.

Heading towards us.

CHAPTER 24

It was like some kind of waking nightmare.

The entire village was marching towards us silently.

I moved nearer to the stage and to the people there who were, I was certain, the only people I could trust; the only people I could rely on now.

We put up our hands and volunteered to be a part of Danny's act, and from that moment on we were set along a different path from the rest of the people of Millgrove.

Call it "chance," "fate," "karma" or "luck," the end result was the same.

We were screwed.

Royally screwed.

I counted the front row of people approaching and there was a straight line of twenty. With twenty behind them. And twenty behind them. Keep repeating until you reach a thousand.

They came across the green towards us, perfectly synchronized.

I recognized every face. People I loved. People I just said hi to. People I didn't like but still managed a smile when I saw them. People I'd done odd jobs for to raise extra pocket money. People I had bought things from. People who had taught me. People I had played with.

I had an impulse to run, to turn and flee, just like Lilly and I had done earlier, but there was another part of me that was tired and scared and just wanted to know what was going on.

Then I wanted it to end.

If that meant aliens were going to take over my mind too then, actually, so be it.

I just couldn't take it anymore. Whatever the crowd wanted of me, I think I was probably prepared to give it to them.

In that moment I had given up.

The crowd was close now. Very close, moving towards us like a single entity, like flocking birds or marching army ants.

Still silent.

And in the front row was my mother; my father; my brother; Dr. Campbell; Mr. and Mrs. Dartington; Simon; Mrs. Carlton, the local busybody; Len Waites, the butcher; Eddie Crichton, who'd never got to hand out a prize at the talent show; Mr. and Mrs. Parnese, who had a stall selling mobile phone accessories on Cambridge Market; Laura Jones, who was a year behind me at school; Peter Parker, who was a librarian, not Spider-Man; a red-faced man I knew by sight, but not by name; Barry and Dennis Geary, the nearest thing to bad boys you got in Millgrove; Karl Raines, the best soccer player at our school; Ellie What's-her-name, barmaid at the Blue Nun in Crowley; some bloke that is always hanging around her like a faithful puppy.

They stopped about three meters away from us.

Perfectly in sync.

Perfectly silent.

They were looking at us, and they were looking *through* us, at the same time. A thousand people in a block.

Lilly took hold of my hand and her palm was cold, her hand was shaking. I held it tight and drew strength from that simple gesture.

We stood there together, facing the crowd, waiting for them to make their move.

CHAPTER 25

Kate O'Donnell took a step forwards.

"What do you want from us?" she demanded.

There was no answer. The crowd just stood there. It was almost as if they had been frozen again.

"They're not even blinking," Lilly whispered.

It was true.

They weren't blinking. Or breathing, it seemed. They weren't moving at all.

"What do you want?" Kate screamed this time. She looked red-faced and terrified.

Again, nothing.

The crowd seemed to be ignoring us.

They were just standing there.

Kate jumped from the stage and homed in on Dr. Campbell.

"All right, you idiot quack," she said spitefully. "Tell me what the hell is going on!"

She put her face just centimeters from the doctor's face and screamed, *"Tell me!"*

She was so close that he must have *felt* her words on his face.

But he didn't appear to flinch.

Kate let out a sound of frustration and sank to her knees, like all the air had been let out of her. I could hear her sobbing. I even felt like joining her. Lilly's hand tightened its grip on mine, and her fingernails bit into the meat of my palm.

Then I heard it.

A low sound that could have been the thrum of an electrical power source, except it seemed to be coming from the crowd of people in front of us. I realized it had been building for a while, but that I had only just become aware of it. It was a deep throbbing sound I could *feel* throughout my body.

I was vibrating along with the noise.

I felt on the very brink of panic, and still the sound continued to develop, getting louder and deeper and making my body vibrate even more, like the heavy bass you get at a rock concert when the PA is really kicking.

Lilly let go of my hand and put her hands up to cover her ears.

"What is that?" she said loudly to compete with the sound that was rising up around us.

The crowd still didn't move.

They just stood there.

"My God." Kate's voice was quiet and full of fear. "Look."

She was still on her knees, and she was staring at Dr. Campbell in front of her. I looked over but couldn't see what she meant.

"His *hands*!" she said. "Oh, God, look at his *hands*!"

I thought she had lost her mind.

And then I looked at Dr. Campbell's hands.

And then I thought maybe I had lost mine.

EDITOR'S NOTE

Kyle pauses here and creates a silence that lasts almost a whole minute. Sounds of breathing can be discerned, but nothing else.

Bernadette Luce has written much about this pause. In "The Importance of What Isn't There: Finding Truth in the Gaps," she hypothesizes about the reason for this pause, deciding, after a particularly long discourse, that "(T)his is the moment where the power of silence overtakes the weakness of language. Kyle Straker, with his silence, tells us all we need to know about this part of the greater narrative. That it is beyond words, it transcends language, and the gap he leaves as he attempts to find a way to describe what happens next are a silent scream that we hear echoing through the rest of the tape. Gaps always provide a good environment for the manufacture of echoes."

The fact that Kyle then manages to describe what he saw when he looked at Dr. Campbell's hands seems to be ignored by Luce.

CHAPTER 26

At first I thought it was a trick of the light.

With the sun starting its climb down from its high point in the sky towards a resting place on the horizon, it *could* have been the result of light and shadow across his skin.

But it was nothing to do with the light, and all to do with the physical appearance of the doctor's hands. The skin of his hands was shifting, as if moved by ripples across its surface, or currents below. It was like the skin itself had suddenly become *capable of moving*, and it wasn't using muscles to do it, it was doing it itself.

As I watched in a horrified fascination, a sudden rush of tiny bumps spread across his skin like a rash. It looked a little like gooseflesh, and before long there were thousands of the bumps covering his skin.

Each bump was crowned with a tiny black dot.

The doctor didn't seem to notice, he just stood there, utterly still while the rash seemed to harden upon the surface of his skin and then, suddenly, began to disgorge thin, whiplike threads from each of the bumps. Skin-colored and minutely thin, these threads sprayed out of the dot at the center of each bump, like water under pressure, or pink Silly String from a can. Each thread, or filament, was ten to fifteen centimeters long, and seemed able to support itself, standing out from his flesh like thin, hard fibers.

The filaments began to stretch, pulling themselves farther from the bumps that housed them, adding twenty centimeters to their length with every second that passed.

The bass vibration deepened again in the air around us.

The filaments on the doctor's left hand were reaching out towards the person next to him.

My dad.

The fibers were moving towards my dad's hand and I had an urge to swat at them, to keep them away from him, to stop them touching him.

Except I didn't want them touching me.

And then it was too late.

The filaments seemed to sense their proximity to Dad's hand and homed straight in on it, flailing at the back of his hand and then sticking to it. Where each filament touched, a bump appeared, identical to the bumps that had spread across the doctor's own skin.

The pores of the bumps opened to accept the filaments, before sucking them inside and sealing themselves closed.

The doctor's hand was now linked to my dad's hand by hundreds—maybe thousands—of flesh-colored threads.

The bass sound ceased abruptly.

"What are they *doing*?" Lilly asked with disgust in her voice.

"They're mutating," Kate O'Donnell said.

I shook my head.

Things started coming together in my head.

Digital code. Data. Computer code as a means of invasion. Thin flesh-colored threads. Fiber-optic cables.

"Not mutating," I said. "Connecting."

C H A P T E R 27

Three simple words.

"Not mutating. Connecting."

The keys that started unlocking the puzzle.

Of course it wasn't until we reached the barn that it all came together. . . . But now I'm doing what I have been avoiding: I'm getting ahead of myself.

It's all starting to blur together, and the pieces are starting to bleed in over other pieces. I have to keep it together.

So you'll know.

So you'll understand.

CHAPTER 28

When things start moving, they can *really* start moving.

We were still reacting to the bizarre sight of the doctor and my dad connecting when suddenly everyone in the crowd was at it.

Filaments began spreading from person to person, to the right, to the left, behind and in front, connecting the crowd into a vast network, bound together by those unnatural fibers.

As a group we stepped back, edging away from the sight before us.

Dr. Campbell was blinking in a definite pattern of blinks—two quick, one slow, three very quick indeed, two slow, then a lot of fluttering blinks, then the whole pattern repeated again—*and every member of the crowd did exactly the same thing at exactly the same time.* Connected by those terrible fleshy fibers, the crowd was now utterly in sync.

We turned and walked away from them.

I don't know about the others, but I didn't even look back.

No one followed.

We headed out of the village, along the High Street. We were driven by an impulse to get as far away from the village green as we could, and it was a few minutes before any of us managed to speak.

So we carried on, along the road that led out to Crowley, and eventually on to Cambridge.

Finally, as pavement faded out to grass verge beneath our feet, Kate O'Donnell managed to speak.

"We're nothing to them," she said helplessly. "Absolutely nothing."

"Then we'll get help," Mr. Peterson told her. "The police. The army. Someone."

"That's if there's anyone left," Lilly said. "What if it's not just Millgrove? What if it's Crowley? And Cambridge? And London? Paris? New York? What if it's *everybody*? Who's going to help us then?"

On either side of us spread the countryside, with fields and trees and hedges. It seemed too ordinary, too normal, for anything to be truly wrong.

Birds sang in the trees and swooped across the landscape.

Grasshoppers and crickets leapt from the grass as we passed.

It all looked so peaceful, so tranquil, so safe.

But the road was quieter than I had ever seen it, and that made the stillness seem artificial, sinister. There were no cars driving in from Crowley, or Cambridge, or from anywhere at all. Perhaps the thing we were fleeing *was* widespread.

But still we walked.

There was nothing else to do.

The sky was reddening on the horizon as the sun sank in the sky, setting the clouds on fire as it went, and we walked towards that horizon.

CHAPTER 29

Twin towers pulled me out of my downward mental spiral.

I saw them silhouetted against the bloodied sky and stopped dead in my tracks. Lots of things suddenly collided inside my head, adding up, making some weird kind of sense.

Old man Naylor's grain silos.

A couple of hundred meters away.

Lilly stopped next to me and followed my gaze. Out of the corner of my eye I saw her face, lined by the red of the setting sun.

"Isn't that where . . . ?" she asked, trailing off to avoid having to finish the sentence with the science-fiction stuff she hated.

I nodded.

"UFO central," I said.

"But Robbie Knox and Sally Baker made that story up to

get attention," Lilly said. She paused and then asked, "Didn't they?"

I shrugged.

Yes, they probably did just make it up.

They said they saw bright lights hovering over one of the silos. Not helicopters. Not planes.

Everyone said that they weren't the type to make up a story like that, but Simon and I had seen the way it had made them minor celebrities among their peers.

"What are you thinking?" Lilly asked. "That maybe the UFOs were the first phase of all this? That maybe there's some link there?"

To tell the truth, I don't know what I was thinking. It just made that weird kind of sense to me. It might have been nothing more than a bizarre coincidence, but maybe "coincidence" was a name given to things by people who just haven't spotted a connection yet.

Kate and Mr. Peterson had joined us and were looking at the silos too.

"I've never liked those things," Kate said. "I've always thought they were incredibly ugly."

She had a point. Like concrete lighthouses without lights to burn or ships to warn, the silos were local landmarks that probably featured in most travel directions given to non-locals. They were dull and gray and rose far above anything else.

"I think we should take a closer look," Lilly said.

It was kind of nice that she had faith in one of my hunches.

Kate O'Donnell shook her head.

"And why would we want to look at a couple of grain silos?" she asked, a sarcastic tone creeping into her voice. "Unless we're saying that Kyle's *alien invasion* is suddenly wheat-based?"

"Er . . . because it might be important." Lilly's response was sarcastic too.

"It sounds more like a wild-goose chase to me," Kate said crossly. "I say we keep walking, see how far this phenomenon extends."

Lilly pursed her lips, put her hands on her hips.

"And I say we go and check out a possible lead," she said firmly.

"A *lead*?" Kate said. "What is this? An American cop show?"

I thought it might be time to intervene.

"Look," I said, "Why don't you and Mr. Peterson wait here. Lilly and I will go and check out the silos. It's probably nothing, but . . ."

"But?"

"There might be an answer there," I finished. "Something other than grain."

Kate shook her head.

"We'll give you fifteen minutes," she said. "Then Rodney and I are walking."

"Fair enough," I said, then turned to Lilly. "You up for this?"

"Of course," she said, and we set out towards the concrete towers.

CHAPTER 30

The sky was darkening, it seemed, with every step we took down the rutted track that led to Naylor's farm. Empty fields stretched around us on each side and I suddenly felt very vulnerable and afraid.

There was probably nothing waiting at the end of this side-quest, but that wasn't the point. At least we were doing something.

I think Lilly felt this sense of purpose too.

"Do you even *believe* in UFOs?" she asked me.

"Sure," I said. "It just means the flying object was *unidentified*. It doesn't necessarily mean there are aliens aboard."

She tutted.

"What?"

"I just wanted to know if you thought we were going to find anything, you know, *weird*, in those silos."

It seemed that as soon as Lilly's words were out there was a sudden, uncanny glow from up ahead. It wasn't even full dark yet, more like a murky twilight, but we could see a sickly light shining brighter than the air around it, a light that seemed . . . *different* . . . to any light I had seen before. It seemed *grainy*, somehow, as if it were made of particles in the air up ahead.

We stopped in our tracks and looked ahead.

Instinctively I put a protective arm around Lilly's shoulders. When I realized what I had done I was half expecting her to throw me off, or to say something sarcastic, but she didn't do either.

So I hugged her to me, wishing that things were different between us.

When we got out of this—*if* we got out of this—I would try to make things up to her.

I squeezed her shoulder and we walked towards the light.

CHAPTER 31

Light is supposed to be reassuring. You learn that when you're very young. It defeats the bad things creeping around in your room.

Every parent knows the magic gesture that chases the monsters away.

Click.

Let there be light.

Here, though, light was kind of the problem. It looked wrong and I suddenly remembered what Mr. Peterson had said earlier, about things from this world looking like they belonged on this world; that they followed rules that allowed us to recognize them, allowed us to understand them.

It had sounded like mad ravings at the time, but now I knew exactly what he had been talking about.

The light we were walking into didn't look as if it belonged here at all.

I had no idea how we should be approaching the silos, how much stealth we needed.

In the end, however, we just walked perfectly normally towards them.

Ordinarily, light illuminates pretty much everything in its path, but this seemed more selective in its illumination. It clumped around objects and highlighted them, while leaving empty areas relatively dark.

Intelligent light? I remember thinking. *How is that even possible?*

"Look," Lilly said, and showed me her arm. "Look at this."

I could see Lilly's bare arm, but I could see more than that. The particles of light had clustered around her limb and I could see dark lines running along the skin, branching off, connecting to other lines, filling Lilly's arm.

Then it became clear to me exactly what the light was showing me and I felt a little sick.

I was seeing *through* Lilly's skin to the veins and arteries beneath. I looked closer and could even see the blood pumping through her.

"You have to admit," Lilly said, "that this is pretty damned cool."

I nodded, suddenly mute.

"I reckon we're in the right place," she said. "Let's go get a look inside those silos."

CHAPTER 32

We were about twenty meters from the first of the silos when a group of people arrived around the corner in front of us, heading the same way. I gestured for Lilly to get out of sight and jogged for cover at the side of the yard.

As the group drew closer to us I realized that I knew most of them. Five members of the Naylor family, including old man Naylor himself, were leading a young woman towards the silo.

Lilly was pointing at the young woman, mouthing something, but there was a rushing sound in my ears and a cold, leaden feeling moving swiftly down my spine.

I recognized her.

I recognized her all too well.

I'd lived next door to her my whole life.

It was Annette Birnie, Danny's sister.

She didn't look like she was doing too well. Her hair, normally straight and neat and perfectly arranged, was a wild, tangled mess, and the face it framed was pale and drawn. Dark skin ringed her eyes. She was moving in a halting fashion, as if she was in shock, and every few steps one of the Naylor family would push her forwards to hurry her up.

"She's one of us," Lilly whispered with horror in her voice. "She's one of the zero-point-four and she's been alone since it happened. We had each other, Kate O'Donnell, Mr. Peterson. She had no one. No one at all."

I knew that Lilly was right and felt a horrible pang of sympathy. To have been completely alone through all of this, I couldn't even begin to think how that must have felt. She must have thought she was losing her mind.

"We should have found her, helped her," Lilly said.

"We didn't know," I said. "We just didn't know."

"Danny hypnotized her too," Lilly said crossly. "We *should* have known."

"He hypnotized her days ago," I countered. "Why would that have affected her today?"

Lilly shook her head.

"We have to help her," she said, and there was a steely tone to her voice that told me she wasn't taking no for an answer.

"If you've got a plan, I'm all ears," I said.

"I distract them, you save Annette," she said as if it was

the easiest thing in the world she was laying out. "Just like in one of your comic books."

"You read comic books?"

"No, but when we're out of this I'll let you show me a couple of comic books to convince me they're worth my time. Deal?"

"Deal."

"Now stay here. I'll get them looking the other way."

"I should be doing that part of the plan."

She shook her head.

"Annette knows and trusts you." She smiled wickedly. "She has a lower opinion of me."

"Sounds like there's some history between you."

"There's always history. You know that. Now let's do this."

"You take care of yourself," I said, but it didn't seem like enough, and then I was leaning forwards, taking her face in my hands, and kissing her on the lips.

She kissed back and then it was over and we were both standing there, wondering what had just happened.

"A kiss for luck?" she said.

"We'll call it that for now," I said breathlessly. "Now go. Distract. We've got a friend to rescue."

CHAPTER 33

Lilly clung to the shadows and made her way quickly up the side of the yard, past a row of dilapidated barns, while I just stood there waiting for a chance to get to Annette. I could still feel the ghost impression of Lily's lips upon mine.

The Naylor family procession had paused next to the closest silo and old man Naylor was standing in front of the structure. He extended his arms before him and a whole load of those weird filaments tore loose from his hands and adhered to the front of the silo. Suddenly, the surface of the structure started to glow, then peel back, creating an opening, then a door.

Hell of a way to make an entrance, I thought, and then the new door swished aside.

The alphabet of hooks and eyes that we saw on Kate O'Donnell's computer were floating in the air inside the silo, as if they were being projected onto the air itself. They twisted and curled and looked sort of brownish to my eyes. But even as I thought the word *brownish*, I realized that was about a million miles away from describing the actual color.

I watched in fascination as the characters of that alphabet changed and mutated before my eyes. I was wondering how it was possible that there could be a language written across the air, and I felt myself taking a step forwards, towards the silo, against my will, as if my body had suddenly broken through of my mind's control.

I felt my foot rising up to take another step. I couldn't stop it.

And I couldn't take my eyes off the symbols in the silo.

My foot took another step.

I knew that I would be in the sight line of the Naylor family any second, but my body still wasn't listening. I felt my foot readying itself for another step.

No. No. No, I tried to tell my foot.

The foot started moving again.

"Hey!" I heard Lilly's voice and it snapped me out of it. I managed to drag my eyes away from the contents of the silo and my foot back from its forwards course.

I saw the Naylors turn to find the source of the interruption and there she was, Lilly, standing about fifty meters away in the middle of the yard, hands on her hips. I actually smiled when I saw her, she looked so composed and . . . well, *heroic,* I guess.

I saw the Naylor clan react to her arrival with surprise and old man Naylor even stepped away from the silo towards her. His . . . *filaments* retracted so fast that their movement was a blur.

Annette just stood there looking dazed and lost.

"Hey!" Lilly shouted again. "Any of you weirdos know where a zero-point-four can get a bed for the night?"

The Naylors looked at her and seemed to confer, although I'm not convinced any of them actually spoke. Then old man Naylor nodded his head towards Lilly.

I sucked in a deep breath and readied myself.

The Naylors started towards her but she stood her ground. I felt proud and sick and scared. The Naylors kept moving towards her, and for a horrible couple of seconds I thought the old man was going to stay behind to guard Annette, but then he followed the rest of his clan, and together they moved in on Lilly.

They were thirty meters away.

Then they were twenty-five.

Then twenty.

It was showtime.

I broke from the shadows, hunched down, and hurried over to Annette Birnie. She was staring into the silo, her eyes filled with the uncanny alphabet within, and I had to physically touch her on the shoulder to get her to notice me.

"Annette," I said calmly. "It's me. Kyle. I'm here to help you. To get you away from here."

She looked at me blankly. For a moment I thought she didn't even recognize me. Then her eyes seemed to show a sudden awareness and her brow furrowed with confusion.

"Kyle?" she asked almost robotically. "What are you doing here?"

"We have to get out of here," I said. "There's no time to explain. But there are more of us. There's me and Lilly and Mrs. O'Donnell and Mr. Peterson. We know what's happened. We want to help you."

"Help me?" Annette's gaze met mine and I saw that there were tears in her eyes. "No. There's no help. There is only . . . *in there*." She pointed at the silo.

"I really don't think you want to go in there, Annette," I said.

I sneaked a quick look over to where the Naylors had almost reached Lilly.

"You want me?" I heard her yell. *"Then you're going to have to catch me!"*

She turned and ran away from them, deeper into the darkness of the farm.

Time was running out.

"Please," I said. "Come with me."

Annette shook her head. Her eyes were wide and all pupils. She looked helpless and defeated.

"In there I can become one of them," she said slowly as if explaining something very simple to a rather dull child. "In there it all ends."

"You don't want to be one of *them*," I said.

"Yes. Yes I do." Annette Birnie looked at me and I saw all the fear that was running through her head, through the dark windows of her eyes. "I don't want to be alone."

I was aware that I was using up all the time Lilly had bought me, but I really hadn't planned for the contingency of Annette not wanting to come with me. I'd thought that she'd be looking for a way to escape, not looking forward to joining them.

Another glance over told me that the Naylors weren't going to give chase. They were standing, looking into the distance, but they weren't following Lilly.

"You won't be alone," I said in what I thought was a soothing voice. "Come on, we can help you."

"Help me?" she said in a puzzled voice. "How do you know what I *want*?"

The question baffled me.

"Look," I said, taking her arm and trying to drag her away from the silo. "Just come with me—"

She didn't let me finish.

"No!" she said, and she said it very loudly.

So loudly it attracted the attention of the Naylors.

Time had completely run out.

The Naylors had spotted me and were making their way back towards us.

"You want to be like them?" I asked, a cruel note in my voice.

Annette's tears came thick and fast now.

"That's all I ever wanted," she said, and turned on her heel. Before I could stop her she moved into the silo.

The moment she entered its proximity, the alphabet seemed to sense she was there. I watched, terrified, as the characters started to twist and flex through the air towards her, the hooks extending to reach her with something that looked like hunger.

"Annette!" I screamed, but she didn't appear to hear me.

Instead, she threw her arms apart and made a cross shape of her body—like a sacrifice—and then the hooks and eyes and squiggles and lines closed in around her, superimposing their alien message over her. At first they fizzed and skated across her skin, and then they stopped moving and seemed to sink into her flesh.

There was a smile on her face as her body absorbed the letters of that terrible language, and I think that scared me more than anything else I was seeing.

Her smile.

I turned and ran, back the way Lilly and I had come.

CHAPTER 34

Lilly caught up with me before I made it back to the road. She wasn't even out of breath.

"Where's Annette?" she asked.

I shook my head.

"She wouldn't come," I said. "She actually *wanted* to become one of them."

I thought Lilly would be angry that I hadn't persuaded Annette to come, but instead she just nodded.

"I guess she finally found a way to fit in. . . ."

I looked at her blankly.

"A few years ago me and Annette were at camp together. Girl Guides, if you must know, but tell anyone else and you're dead.

"Anyway, long story short and all that, we kind of paired up while we were there. We were talking one night, out under the stars, and it was probably *because* we weren't really friends that she confided in me.

"She told me about how she had never felt like she fit in, that there was this huge weight of expectation that everyone put on her, but that no matter how hard she tried she always felt like an outsider, an impostor, a fake. She'd even thought about killing herself because she couldn't bear the idea of going through life alone.

"Nothing I said helped, and after camp she never spoke to me again. She showed me a part of herself that was secret, and it would have got in the way if I'd been the one to approach her."

Lilly took a deep breath and continued.

"You did your best, Kyle. You're a nice guy, you know that?"

She gave me a smile, but I didn't feel like a nice guy.

A nice guy would have found a way to save Annette.

"So the silo can turn us into one of them?" Lilly said. "Are you tempted?"

I shook my head.

"Not even hardly," I said.

Lilly raised an eyebrow.

"My parents were barely getting along," I explained. "Now it's like nothing ever happened to disturb their happiness."

"Is that so bad?"

"Not if you like lies so much you want to live one," I

snapped. "My dad ran off, and I don't see why we should forget it. Forgive it? Sure, we could do that. But *forget*? Forget the sadness he caused? That would be plain wrong."

"You think that sadness is better than happiness?"

"No. But it is important."

"Because we learn from it?" Lilly asked.

I nodded.

"The real question is: do we tell the others?" I said.

"Tell them what?"

"That they just have to go to Naylor's farm and the nightmare's over for them."

"There are few enough of us around as it is," Lilly said. "Why on earth would we want to tell them that?"

A secret then.

Shared between Lilly and me.

I liked that.

We walked down the road to meet the other two.

CHAPTER 35

We joined up with the others and we told our lie.

Nothing happened, we said.

It almost made me want to retract the lie when Kate O'Donnell gave us a triumphant I-told-you-so look, but Lilly and I had made our pact of silence, so we just fell into step with her and Mr. Peterson and carried on down the road.

My stomach felt empty and hollow and I wished one of us had the foresight to bring some kind of provisions along. It had been a long time since I had last eaten.

That made me think of the second can of Red Bull, and I put my hand in my pocket to pull it out. There was a dull, metallic sound as if the can had hit against something in the pocket, but I didn't think about it at the time, because I was already greedily pulling the ring pull and taking a couple of sips. I handed the can to Lilly and she smiled, drank a bit, handed it back.

I offered the can to the adults—Mr. Peterson took a drink, Kate just frowned at the can and shook her head—and we kept on walking.

It was Mr. Peterson who heard it first.

I turned around and saw that he had stopped in the middle of the road behind us. He had his head cocked to the left and was cupping his ear with his hand. I motioned to Lilly and Kate and walked back to where he was standing.

"You okay there, Mr. P?" I asked.

He looked exhausted, his face red and blotchy, dark shadows under his eyes, and his graying hair was sticking out at strange angles.

"Can you hear it?" he asked in a breathless voice, and he sounded so earnest and . . . and *afraid* I guess, and it contrasted with the silly cupped ear thing that I almost burst out laughing.

Almost.

But then I heard it too.

Lilly and Kate had joined us but I hardly noticed them arrive.

I was listening to the sound.

That is if *sound* is the right word for it. Because it seemed like it was made up of a lot of sounds: a high-pitched hiss like gas escaping at pressure from a ruptured pipe; an insectile *chitter* like a locust swarm; that deep, bass vibration we'd heard in the village; a high, keening wail.

It sounded distant.

But not that distant.

Certainly not distant enough.

And I realized that I had heard the sound before, back at Kate O'Donnell's house, just before she shut her computer down.

"What *is* that?" Kate asked.

"Nothing good," I said.

The noise drew closer.

I'm not exaggerating, my skin bristled with gooseflesh.

There was something about the sound that hit me at a primal level, like the sound of a tyrannosaur must have put the fear into a tiny mammal that stumbled into its killing grounds.

Closer, the sound was terrifying.

It sounded like something was out there in the half-light, getting closer and closer to us with every passing second. Something awful, something dangerous, something that we could not even *begin* to imagine the shape or size of.

We started walking, moving away from the sound. It was all there was to do. Whatever was out there was coming after *us*, I was certain.

Lilly's walking pace speeded up, and we all matched her speed.

Everyone's face reflected their fear.

Fear of whatever was making that sound.

Getting closer with every second.

CHAPTER 36

We ran.

A jog became a run became a sprint and still that sound was close on our heels.

My eyes were squeezed shut and I had stopped thinking of anything except that noise behind us.

Suddenly, I realized: the noise was *no longer* behind us.

It was to the side of us.

Running parallel to the road, across the fields, shadowing us.

Running parallel to us.

Running to overtake us.

Except, of course, *running* isn't the right word for it at all. Sure, I could hear it crashing through the undergrowth at great speed, but there were no footsteps. Just this weird phasing static that was more like some stereo-panning effect from a video game than an actual sound in the real world.

I opened my eyes and started scanning the hedges by the side of the road for a sign of the thing that was making such a terrible noise. I could see nothing there, and that made me even more terrified. I ran faster.

I've never been particularly athletic, but I think I could have run for the Olympics if I'd matched the speed I was making then, spurred on by that inhuman sound.

I was even starting to feel that I might outrun it.

Suddenly, Lilly screamed my name.

CHAPTER 37

The sound pulled me back to the real world.

I turned my head to face forwards.

Just in time.

I killed the speed. Ground to a halt and stood there, gasping for air.

I realized that Lilly had just saved my life.

The thing that had been following us, then moving alongside us, had now overtaken us.

It was waiting there, directly in front of me.

Blocking my way forwards.

It's not easy to describe it. In fact, the more I think about it, it's probably easier to talk about what this thing *wasn't*, than to struggle with what it was. I mean, I don't think the thing was solid, and I'm reasonably sure that it didn't have a form that the human eye could recognize. It didn't look alive, but it didn't look *not*-alive, either. It didn't look *natural*, but it didn't look entirely *unnatural*.

Oh, yeah, I'm making a good job of this.

Let me try again.

It seemed more like *something missing* from this world, than something added to it. It was as if there were a tear in the skin of our world, and it had revealed this terrible thing beneath it.

At the time, I remember thinking about those pictures you see in anatomy books, when they show a person, and then the bones and muscles inside them.

You strip away the skin of this world, I thought, *and this is what you find hiding underneath.*

"What in God's name is it?" Kate O'Donnell asked, and I saw her cross herself.

I shook my head.

It was too much.

This tear in the world had been following us, hunting us, and now it had us.

And we were too tired and too scared to do anything about it.

It moved closer, pushing against the surface of our world and making the air seem to bulge as it did. I stood there wondering what stuff this . . . *thing*, this tear was made of, and I wondered what it would do to us when it reached us: whether it would hurt; whether it would dissolve us, melt us, or suck us through into its cold blackness until we were nothing.

There were tears streaming down my cheeks, and I could feel the cold breath of infinity roaring in my face.

"Hey!" someone shouted from somewhere behind me. "Are you going to just stand there and let that thing wipe you off the face of the planet?"

I turned around.

Somehow I wasn't surprised.

By the side of the road, standing straight and tall, stood Danny. He nodded towards the tear in space and cocked his head to one side.

"If you have any interest in surviving the next few seconds," he said, "then I suggest you toss over that video camera you picked up on the green."

I thought, *The video camera? What is he talking about?*

The air bulged again and the tear moved closer.

I thought, *How does he know I'm carrying his mum's video camera?*

Danny said, "Quickly. Throw it here."

I reached down and fumbled the camera out of my pocket. Lights were flashing on its tiny casing.

It had switched itself on when the can of drink hit it.

It had been filming the inside of my pocket all that time.

"Do it now," Danny advised, and I threw it over to him. He caught it in one hand and switched it off.

Then he smiled and nodded towards the tear in space. It was already drawing back, moving away, as if its interest in us—the interest that had it screaming across the countryside—had suddenly ended.

"Danny, what the—?" I started, but Danny shut me up with a dismissive wave of his hand.

"I guess you all have questions," Danny said, and his face suddenly looked sad. "Follow me and I'll try to answer some of them for you."

Then the sad look was gone.

He turned and started walking into the field behind him, away from that terrible patch of moving darkness, away from the road, away from Millgrove, away from Crowley.

After a few seconds, we followed.

We trudged across a field sun-baked into clay, following Danny Birnie in pursuit of answers. Danny had been there at the start of all this, and there was something *right* about his being here now.

I realized that I was afraid. Not of the terrible thing that had been seconds away from destroying us, but afraid of my friend.

Of Danny.

Of what he had become.

He walked quickly, neither slowing down nor turning to check that we were keeping up with him. Or if we were even following him, for that matter.

The sky was almost full dark now, with a summer-stuffed moon looming on the horizon, surrounded by wisps of cloud and tiny, icy chips of starlight.

For centuries humankind had stared up into a sky like that and wondered whether they were alone in the universe.

Now I thought we had our answer.

A dark, tall shape loomed out of the darkness ahead of us and Danny led us towards it. Eventually the shape resolved itself out of the near dark, revealed itself to be an old, ramshackle barn on the edge of the field.

"I guess here is as good as anywhere," Danny said.

He walked into the barn.

It was no longer Danny, I was certain of that. He was *one of them*. This could be a trap, an ambush, a massacre.

But he might *really* have answers.

Answers we needed.

We followed him into the barn.

Quietly.

Like cattle.

Or . . .

EDITOR'S NOTE

The last break in the narrative as the end of the tape once more gets in the way. Howard Tillinghast sees this break as crucial: "This is the point at which innocence breathes its last gasp of oxygen, before revelation takes it away, forever."

. . . last side of the last tape I can find. It's one of Dad's mix tapes that he makes for the car so he can embarrass us with his bizarre musical taste on long journeys.

Still, I guess we're almost through now. There's not a whole lot more to tell.

Only the bad stuff.

The stuff I don't even want to think about.

This might get a little mixed up, but bear with me, I need to work out the best way to tell you the things I have to tell you.

I wonder if anyone's listening.

If you are, then I need you to believe me.

It's the truth.

CHAPTER 38

Inside the barn it was dark, and there was a musty stench in the air that made me gag. My shin crashed into something hard.

"Oh, I'm sorry," Danny said in the gloom. "How thoughtless of me."

I heard him moving about and then . . .

. . . then it wasn't dark any longer.

I heard Kate O'Donnell gasp.

Oh, I know how crazy this sounds. Do you know how many times I have run it through in my head and still end up doubting the evidence of my own senses?

An eerie halo of reddish light, bright enough to illuminate the barn around us, suddenly appeared, surrounding Danny.

He smiled.

"Bioluminescence," he said as if it was another of his conjuring tricks he was performing and he was particularly proud of it. "Knew I could do it, but . . . well . . . *wow!*"

Danny looked at us and shrugged.

"It's a simple trick, really," he said. "Basically, I converted some skin cells to photoproteins." He spoke as if that was not only normal, but something we should understand. "I'm fueling them with some excess calcium that I'm growing from my own skeleton."

NOTE—*"Bioluminescence"*

Although dramatically simplified, this is indeed the way that we produce light. One of the strengths of the Straker tapes is, I believe, that they do show us the things we do normally and naturally in a new and different way, as if Kyle is really experiencing these commonplace sights for the first time, in the position of an outsider.

In "Identity Crises: Bodies as Text," Steinmetz writes: "Things we take for granted are shown in a new light by Straker's words. Filament networking and bioluminescence are so familiar to us that it takes a boy to remind us how precious these things are."

He laughed.

"It tickles, if anyone's interested."

We stood there openmouthed, trying to work out if Danny was toying with us, or whether he'd really just used parts of his skeleton to light up the barn.

There was a long silence and then Lilly stepped towards Danny with a ferocious look on her face that was altered into something satanic by that strange red glow. Danny shook his head, and there was something about the way that he did it that made Lilly stop in her tracks.

Suddenly, it wasn't rage on her face.

It was fear.

One small shake of the head and that's what Danny could do now: stop rage and turn it into fear.

What have you done with my friend? I thought, because this wasn't him.

"Please," Lilly said. "Please, Danny. Stop playing around with us. I've had enough. I'm tired and cold and scared and I want to go home. What happened today? Why has everyone . . . *changed*? What are you?"

Danny looked on the verge of saying something. He had a dreadfully serious expression on his face and seemed to be having trouble finding the right words. Instead he looked around the barn and gestured towards a row of straw bales at the back of the barn.

"Okay," he said. "Sit down."

"We don't want to sit down," Mr. Peterson said crossly. "We want to know what the hell is going on."

"Then sit!" Danny said, his face suddenly looking cruel in the red light.

We sat.

"I only have a few hours," Danny said. "This is a . . . *caretaking routine* for the master program that will end as soon as the installer quits." He paused and reflected on his words.

"Actually, and more accurately, it's a *subroutine*, but that's just splitting hairs."

"The master program," Lilly said. She turned to me. "That's what you were talking about. A computer program that was the spaceships and ray guns all rolled into one. You were *right*."

Danny laughed.

"Was he?" he said, amused by the idea. "Why, Kyle? What did you say?"

His gaze made me feel nervous.

"I said that our planet was being invaded," I said. "That we were experiencing an alien invasion that doesn't waste ships or troops, and doesn't give us a chance to fight back."

Danny raised an eyebrow.

"Sounds fascinating," he said, his voice *dripping* with condescension. "Tell me more."

I felt a sudden, red urge to punch him in the face.

Instead I carried on.

"Whenever I try to get my head around all of this, I keep coming back to computers," I said. "I don't know if it's because we first saw the weird language on Kate's iMac, but it made me realize that an invasion doesn't have to be violent. Because an alien race could send a signal across space, a signal that contained a computer program designed to *overwrite* humanity *and all the things that make us human*. With one clever piece of software they could change us all, at once, into the image of themselves.

"Maybe human DNA has been altered by this signal. And human brains are being reprogrammed to mimic the invaders' brains."

Danny grinned as if he was delighted with my words. He clapped his hands together and then rubbed them against each other.

"Oh, how *delightful*," he said, again with the patronizing tone, the superior air. He was almost daring me to continue.

"We just happened to be in your trance when the signal was transmitted," I said. "A one-in-a-million chance. It meant our brains were in a different state, and the signal passed us over. Maybe our invaders had considered every possible human state—from awake to asleep and everything in between—but hadn't considered *hypnotized*. Maybe there's a tiny percentage of humanity that—for a variety of reasons—will be immune to this *invasion by upgrade*. Us. The zero-point-four."

"Zero-point-four," Danny said, rolling the phrase around his mouth, still obviously amused. "Oh, yes, you are zero-point-four. You must know, or at least sense, that you are no longer . . . *relevant*."

"We feel pretty relevant," Mr. Peterson said.

"Of course you do," Danny said solemnly. "But you're wrong."

"What are you talking about?" Mr. Peterson demanded.

"The problem, as I see it, is that you completely mis-understand the nature of the thing that has happened to you," Danny said. "That has happened to *us*. But how to explain?"

He pretended to be puzzled, then grinned as he pulled Mrs. Birnie's video camera from his pocket.

"Aha," he said. "Exhibit A. The *invasion* captured on amateur video. Have you watched it yet? Oh, silly me, of course you haven't."

He handed the camera to Lilly.

"Just press PLAY," he told her.

Lilly fumbled with the device, pushing buttons again and again, and getting frustrated at her lack of success.

"Hurry. Hurry," Danny said. "Unless you want the *vestigivore* catching up with you again."

He saw our blank looks.

"Ves-ti-gi-vore," he said. "*Vestige*—a sign, mark, indica-tion, or relic. *Vore*—suffix, meaning eater. *Vestigivore*—eater of relics, of things no longer needed. How about you think of it as . . . well, as a kind of *antivirus software*. As in: it touches you and you die, almost as if you never existed. Delete. No restore from recycle bin."

He cocked his head.

"Listen," he said.

The roaring, chattering, hissing sound from earlier suddenly seemed very close.

Just outside the barn, in fact.

"Give me the camera," Danny demanded urgently. "Quickly now."

Lilly threw it back at him as if the object had suddenly grown hot in her hands.

The sound ceased, almost instantaneously, like a switch had been thrown.

Just like the sound had stopped outside Kate O'Donnell's house the moment she turned her computer off. And like it had stopped when I threw the camera to Danny.

"For simplicity's sake, think of it like this," Danny said. "You are . . . have become . . . *incompatible* with this camera. You four are analog. The camera is digital." He turned to Lilly. "The reason you couldn't get it to play is because you can't. It, like me, has been *upgraded*. You might set it off by accident, and incur the wrath of a *vestigivore*, but our technology is pretty much dead to you now."

He pocketed the camera.

"I'll put this somewhere safe," he said.

"What are you talking about?" Kate said. "None of what you are saying makes any sense."

"Well, let me make things clearer," Danny said. "You four just happened to be in a hypnotic trance when the most significant event in history occurred. An upgrade to the human operating system was transmitted, and you missed it." He smiled. "Oops."

I felt my temper rising.

"Wait a minute," I said. "An upgrade? You're saying all of this is happening *because of an upgrade*?"

"Correct," Danny said. "A necessary software update with a raft of improvements, bug fixes, and a whole load of new and interesting features."

The look on our faces made him chuckle. I saw Lilly's jaw was clenched, and her hands were tight fists at her sides. I guess she wanted to punch him too.

"You only have to take a look at the world around you to see the old operating system was hopelessly out-of-date," Danny said in a mocking voice. "Now we have an alternative. From this day everything changes. There will be an end to crime, war, poverty, fear, starvation, disease, greed, and envy; a straight path, fast track, express route into a golden future of unlimited possibilities."

He looked at me with a hint of what I thought might be sadness.

"Unfortunately, you won't be coming on that journey with us," he said. "Oh, there are many more like you; people who just happened to be in the wrong phase of sleep; people driving who got mildly hypnotized by the white lines on the road; people under the influence of certain drugs; people in the grip of near-death experiences; people engaged in certain types of daydreams. Blah blah blah. There's a subsidiary file that lists all this stuff, a sort of ReadMe I guess you'd call it, but the upshot of it is that you won't be *completely* alone."

"Alone?" Lilly said. "What do you mean?"

A cloud seemed to pass across Danny's face. Again, I thought it might be sadness, a trace of regret.

"I guess I really haven't been explaining myself all that well," he said. "We . . . and by that I mean anyone who isn't zero-point-four . . . have, er, been changed. Changed into creatures capable of putting the world to rights. A software upgrade was transmitted and, even though we're still in the early phases of the upgrade, now that we have learned filament networking it should be over in"—he looked at his wrist, even though he wasn't wearing a watch—"a few hours.

"Then no one will even know you are here. You will be filtered out. You will be pieces of old code floating around in a system that no longer recognizes you. You should be okay, as long as you stay away from any digital technology. If you don't, then . . . well, you've seen a *vestigivore*—they are programmed to delete harmful code."

"This is madness," I said.

"This is the *end of madness,* my friend," Danny said. "A new world is being born. Everything is going to be okay."

"But not for us," Lilly said.

Danny shrugged.

"How can we just be filtered out?" I asked, my mouth suddenly dry.

"The human mind filters out all sorts of useless detail," Danny said. "It's how you get through the day without being driven mad. You don't register the things that aren't, for whatever reason, important to you. I don't mean to sound harsh, but that's what you have become to us: useless. Relics. Dinosaurs."

He broke off for a short while, and then he said, "Have you ever seen something out of the corner of your eye, but when you looked there was nothing there? Or felt like you're being watched, when there's no one around? Dead code. Old systems. Things you have been programmed not to see. Occasionally we catch a glimpse. And tell stories of ghosts and monsters. They're what make dogs bark at night, or a cat's hackles rise. They're there, you've just been programmed not to see them."

"That would mean that this has happened before," I said. "That *we* are already upgrades of earlier systems that we were programmed to screen out."

"Well, duh, of course it has and of course we are," Danny said. "Humans are, after all, a work in progress."

"And it's always zero-point-four of the population who miss the upgrade?" Lilly asked him. "I mean that's still a *lot* of people to ignore."

Danny laughed, loud and long, and I felt that I was missing out on the joke.

"Oh, now, that is utterly priceless," Danny said, still laughing. "I see how you made the mistake, but . . . oh, that is just too much."

And then he laughed some more.

"Care to explain the punch line to us?" Mr. Peterson said.

"The humor lies in the fact that you extrapolated from the available data and reached an understandable, but utterly erroneous, conclusion. A village of close to a thousand people, there are four of you . . . oh, it's just hilarious."

He rubbed his hands with glee.

"Zero–point–four isn't a percentage," he said. "It's the *software version number*. You're software version zero–point–four, the rest of us just jumped to one–point–zero."

CHAPTER 39

There was silence while we tried to process all the things that Danny was saying.

It wasn't easy.

No one should have to hear that life, as they know it, has ended.

No one should have to learn that they are, to all intents and purposes, irrelevant.

Yet, out of the madness, one thought just kept nagging at me and I was the one who broke the silence.

"You say that this is the result of a computer program, transmitted with the sole intention of making this planet a better place?" I asked him.

Danny nodded. "Precisely."

"But a transmission requires a transmitter," I said. "So, transmitted by who?"

"Ah," said Danny. "That really is the crucial question, isn't it? Well, I'm sorry. I haven't got a clue. I'm afraid the programmers haven't included themselves as data. That's not really the job of software, is it? It's a bunch of instructions, not a biographical sketch."

"So we're to believe this . . . your version of events, without even knowing who did this to us?" Mr. Peterson asked.

"It really doesn't matter whether you believe it or not," Danny said coldly. "If a person refuses to believe in gravity, it doesn't mean that they will float up into the sky. Science isn't like that. It doesn't care whether you believe it."

He studied his fingernails.

"Anyway, that's not why I'm here," he continued. "I am telling you this so that you have a *chance* at survival. So you understand the nature of what has happened to you, and you understand *why* this is happening to you. I am telling you this so that when the people you know and love simply *stop seeing you*, when the majority of people on this planet become unaware of your existence, then maybe you won't go totally and utterly out of your minds. You have simply become . . . *irrelevant*. You will become invisible to us. That's going to be pretty hard for you to take."

Lilly made a frustrated sound.

"Excuse me?" Danny said. "Did you just interrupt me to snort?"

Lilly looked back at him with cold concentration, almost as if she was trying to outstare him.

"It's not true," she said.

"O-kaaay," Danny said as if talking to a small child. "What isn't true now?"

"Any of this," she said. "It doesn't even make any freaking sense! You can't upgrade humanity and we're not just hardware that you can rewrite. We're the way we are because of millions of years of evolution."

She threw her arms in the air in frustration. "So I am going to explain everything that has happened today without bolting on aliens. Which, by the way, I hate."

"I'm all ears," Danny said.

The red glow seemed to deepen around him, throwing shadows across his face.

"We're still hypnotized," Lilly said. "We're still in a trance. We're standing on the stage on the green and everything else is just fantasy."

She glared at Danny.

"So bring us out of it," she demanded. "Now. Snap your fingers, or whatever it is that you do, and wake us up."

Danny smiled the strangest of smiles.

"I wonder . . . ," he said. "Shall I snap my fingers? Shall I put this . . . hypothesis of yours to the test? Will you awake, back on the stage, with the roar of laughter from the audience ringing in your ears? What do you think?"

As he spoke he lifted his hand into the air, just above his head, his thumb and first two fingers resting together, ready to snap together.

"Here goes," he said.

He brought his hand down and snapped his fingers.

CHAPTER 40

We awoke on the stage, blinking in the bright light of a perfect summer afternoon and everyone was laughing and really amazed by Danny's newfound gift and Danny won the talent show and when we all went home we said it was the best day ever and we laughed about 0.4 and alien operating systems and were amazed by the detail of the fantasy that Danny had constructed for us and—to cut a long story short—we all lived happily ever after.

CHAPTER 41

Except that wasn't what happened.

Of course it wasn't.

That's just silly storybook stuff.

When Danny clicked his fingers, nothing happened.

We were in the barn, Danny was still shining inside his bioluminescent aura, and Mr. Peterson, Lilly, Kate, and I were still very much 0.4.

It was in the silence following the click that things happened.

Small things.

Human things.

The only things we had left.

Lilly started to cry—huge, body-wracking sobs and fat tears—and Kate O'Donnell put a protective arm around her. I just stood, watching dust motes swirling in the air of the barn and tried to find a way through this.

Without falling apart.

Danny stood there, watching us.

Watching us all deal with it as best we could.

He took no pleasure from the sight, I'm pretty sure of that, but watched with a cold, alien detachment that made me wonder if the 1.0 were going to be as perfect as Danny seemed to think.

Maybe he wasn't even really listening. Perhaps the alien code was bedding down, performing last-minute tweaks.

I realized that he was losing interest in us, and started looking more and more like he needed to be somewhere else.

I had a few last questions for Danny.

Danny the boy magician, encased in his impossible halo of bone-fueled light.

I asked Danny what he was leaving out, what he wasn't telling us.

He looked a little baffled.

Maybe a little hurt, although maybe that's just me, trying to see him as my friend, rather than the alien thing he had become.

"That list of people who'd skipped the upgrade," I said. "You said it was contained in a ReadMe file. What is that?"

"It seems to be installation information," he said. "Although for whom, and why, I do not know. I'm sure it will auto-delete when the update is complete."

"What else does it say?" I asked him.

Danny looked surprised that it interested me, but then he

shrugged and started reeling off a bunch of jargon and tech-stuff in a robotic voice before trailing off into silence.

Most of it I didn't understand: so most of it I don't remember.

But I do remember three things he said about halfway through his recitation.

Danny said, "Fixed system slowdown when individual units are put to sleep, allowing greater access to unconscious processing activity."

And he said, "Tightened encrypted storage parameters to comply with new guidelines."

And then he said, "Completely reworked user interface makes access of data easier and faster."

"What does that mean?" I asked when he was finished.

Danny shook his head.

"I'm sure you'll figure it out," he said.

"Why did they leave us here?" I asked. "Why didn't they just get that vestigivore thing to wipe us all out?"

Danny smiled a cryptic smile.

"That wouldn't be anywhere near so entertaining, would it now?" he said.

I thought he was joking.

"I'd say 'I'll be seeing you,'" Danny said. "Except I won't, of course."

Just before he turned for the door, he looked at me and said, "Annette says hi."

I stared back at him.

"She says it was really sweet of you," he said. "Trying to save her and all."

I could sense Kate O'Donnell's stony glare and felt my cheeks redden.

"Now she wants to try to do the same for you," Danny said, that red aura fading. "Meet her up at the Naylor silos and you can end all of this now."

Then he turned and left.

Didn't look back.

A taste of things to come.

CHAPTER 42

"What did he mean?" Kate O'Donnell demanded. "About the silos, and Annette and trying to save her?"

We were sitting on bales of straw, and it was pretty much full dark.

I felt the words knot up on the tip of my tongue.

"Well?" she prompted. "Do you have something to tell us?"

Lilly's hand sought out mine and I held on to it tightly, as I told Kate and Rodney Peterson about what had really happened when we separated on the Crowley Road.

Kate was furious.

"And you didn't think that this might be a piece of information that we would want to know?" she said incredulously. "You selfish, stupid—"

"Steady on, Kate," Mr. Peterson said calmly. "They were only—"

"Only what?" she demanded. "Only keeping things from us? Only telling us lies? Only preventing us from making the most important decision of our life?"

"There's no decision to make," Mr. Peterson said. "I'm not going to volunteer to become one of those . . . *things.*"

There was another silence. A big empty space where nothing was said, but so much was revealed.

It was Mr. Peterson that broke it.

"Surely you're not actually *considering* it?" he asked, his voice shocked.

"I don't know," Kate said at last. "It might not be so bad."

"I *saw* them," Mr. Peterson said firmly. "I saw them for what they really are. I can tell you this with absolute certainty: *they are not the same as us.* Not even close. I saw them and I do not want to be one of them. I'm happy being who I am."

Kate let out a cruel bark of laughter.

"A postman and part-time ventriloquist?" she said derisively. "A *bad* ventriloquist, at that."

Mr. Peterson looked at her, not with anger, but with humor.

"I guess that is who and what I appear to be," he said. "But that doesn't mean it's all I am, or the way it has always been. For now, being a postman is good, honest work. And it makes me happy. Not everyone has to fly high to prove they exist; some of us are perfectly happy flying low and enjoying the view.

"I'll never be rich, but that doesn't matter to me. Before I came to Millgrove I had a good job, a devoted wife, and a beautiful little boy. But leukemia stole my son from me, and everything else just crumbled away. Iain was four when he became ill, and Mr. Peebles was just something silly I made to put a smile on his face. Most of the joke was how bad I was. But when he was laughing he forgot the pain, and that was better than doing nothing and watching him slip away.

"So, yes, I'm a *terrible* ventriloquist, but it used to make Iain laugh. And so once a year I get Mr. Peebles out of the cupboard and I stand in front of the village and I invite everyone to laugh. Not with me, but at me. Hearing other kids laughing makes me think, just for a second, that he's still here. Here in the world. Not a cold, dead thing in the ground.

"I don't want to be upgraded. I don't want to become one of those things. I want to remember my son. If you want to give up, become one of them because it's easier, then go ahead. But difficult is good. It's what makes us human."

"I'm sorry," Kate said quietly. "I'm just scared. More scared than I have ever been."

"Scared is something," Mr. Peterson said.

We sat there in silence, letting it all sink in.

We were all scared, but who wouldn't be?

If what Danny said was true—and I for one no longer had any doubts—then we no longer existed.

We were 0.4.

Irrelevant.

EDITOR'S NOTE

There is a long pause here, followed by an odd acoustic glitch, which Lucas Pauley identifies as the tape being manually stopped. Then there is an odd snatch of music—in which the words "sirens are howling" can be (just about) discerned.

Ella Benison notes a dramatic change between the tape stopping and being restarted: "The tone of Kyle Straker's voice has changed, and is more like the struggling narrative voice we saw during the first passage of the first tape. To me it seems obvious that Kyle needed time to settle back into his narrative flow because the time that has passed from switching off the tape to switching it back on is considerable."

CHAPTER 43

That was all three months ago now.

Three long and very strange months.

I still remember every detail of that crazy day and crazier night.

Now I have committed them to tape I hope the nightmares that replay them every night when I close my eyes might finally leave me in peace.

Or the thing we call peace these days.

Danny didn't lie to us, you see.

If anything, he understated.

We stepped out of the barn when it was morning. It was just before seven a.m. according Mr. Peterson's Mickey Mouse watch. The dawn revealed a low bed of mist that clung to the field, making it seem ghostly.

Lilly and I had done a lot of talking well into the night.

Then we'd lain there on lumpy, scratchy bales of straw and tried to sleep: the kind of fitful half sleep that bends a person's back in such a way that it hurts when you move and it hurts a different way when you don't.

We had a fuzzy-headed vote on what we should do next, and the consensus was that we go back into Millgrove. If a fraction of what Danny said was true, then we wanted to see evidence of it at home.

It seemed important, somehow.

A way to say good-bye to the things we had lost.

We hit the village outskirts and headed in towards the green.

In my mind I had a single plan.

I was going to walk up to someone I knew and I was going to wish them a very good morning.

And as it was early on a Sunday morning, it was likely that the people of Millgrove would still be sleeping, so I reckoned I would have to walk up to a front door, ring a doorbell, and see what happened from there.

As it turned out, things were nothing like we had expected.

CHAPTER 44

If the people of Millgrove had slept, there was certainly no sign of it. As we drew nearer to the green we could see that the place was a hive of activity. From a distance it looked like the people were pulling the village apart. Frantically. Cars, buildings, even lampposts seemed to be in the process of being dismantled.

It looked like some people were digging up areas of the path and road as well.

They were systematically wrecking the village, with wires and cables being ripped from the ground; cars with their bonnets open being stripped of engines and electrical systems; lampposts were opened up and their wires bared; people were knocking holes in the roofs of their houses; teams of locals came out of houses with gadgets and appliances that were then piled up on the village green. Washing machines and fridges; television sets and home computers; lawn mowers and microwave ovens and leaf blowers and electric toasters.

We were starting our first day under *The New Rules.*

NEW RULE NUMBER ONE: Don't try to understand what the 1.0 are doing; you're simply not wired to understand them.

A group of people were working on dismantling the equipment, and putting the components of each item into carefully ordered piles.

The people working on the cars would occasionally walk over and drop components, lightbulbs, or car batteries off at this strange recycling center, where they were quickly and efficiently organized.

There was no idle chatter; no one was messing about or goofing off.

We reached the green and no one even saw us arrive. We stood there watching the crazy industry around us and, if we happened to be in the way, the person who needed to get past would suddenly change their path slightly to avoid us without even a passing glance.

We tried talking to them, pleading with them, screaming at them, but nothing could get them to notice us.

Just like Danny had said.

We were being filtered out.

We were irrelevant to them.

NEW RULE NUMBER TWO: The 1.0 can't see or hear us.

They really can't.

It's not a trick—they're not pretending not to see us—we no longer register to them, and all memory of us has been wiped from their minds.

So we watched for a while, stunned by the activity going on around us. If there was rhyme or reason to what they were doing, then it wasn't a rhyme or a reason we knew.

No matter what we did or said, we could not get them to notice us.

"I've just about had enough of this," Mr. Peterson said angrily. He rolled up his sleeves and walked straight up to Eddie Crichton, who was hauling a dishwasher out onto the green.

I saw what Mr. Peterson planned to do, but I don't think any amount of sensible argument could have stopped him.

He drew back his fist and punched Eddie in the face.

I closed my eyes for a second, not wanting to watch, and I waited for the sound of a fist connecting with a face and maybe a howl of pain.

I got neither.

I opened my eyes.

Mr. Peterson was standing there looking confused.

Eddie Crichton just carried on with what he was doing. It didn't look like he had felt a thing. It didn't look like he had noticed a thing. He dropped off the dishwasher and made his way down the road. Mr. Peterson strode back angrily.

"I couldn't lay a glove on him," he said when he came back. "All the energy I put into the blow . . . it just . . . I don't know . . . *it went somewhere else.*"

Now, of course, three months down the road, we know exactly what Mr. Peterson meant. We can't entirely explain it, but we know it well.

NEW RULE NUMBER THREE: We can't touch the 1.0.

We can't get closer than an inch or so away from them without our hand/body/whatever getting stopped by some force or charge that prevents us making physical contact. It's like some kind of dampening field, a protective layer that means that the 0.4 and the 1.0 are no longer capable of interacting.

Over the course of the day we watched as the people we once knew used the machines of the village to construct strange new technologies, recycling their possessions to create new machines. Often we would see people interface with a machine, a component, a circuit board, by connecting to it with those fleshy filaments.

NEW RULE NUMBER FOUR: You never get used to the sight of those filaments.

You really, really don't.

Of all the things *they* do that seem alien to us, this one is still the worst. It affects you at a base level, both horrifying and captivating at the same time. You *know* it's something you shouldn't see, something that goes against all the laws of nature and order.

But you still find yourself staring.

We sat there on the edge of the green and watched as people suddenly started fusing themselves to circuit boards, changing the chips and connections by what seemed like thought alone.

Even Chris—my baboon boy, idiot, football-obsessed brother—was performing delicate adjustments to the circuitry. Which was such an unlikely sight that I watched him for a long time. And as I sat there, I began to realize that Chris was gone now, gone forever, and that we would never argue or fight again. I felt a cold stab of regret, of loss, and I had to turn away from him.

I was surprised to find that I had tears in my eyes.

Lilly was taking it all rather badly.

She had been growing more and more gloomy, watching as the people acted in ways that were strange and disturbing. I kept trying to reassure her but it didn't work.

Eventually she stood up, made an exasperated noise, and stormed off across the green without another sound. I wondered if I should follow her, but she hadn't invited me and she probably needed some time to work things out by herself.

Kate took off a few minutes later, and Mr. Peterson went with her to make sure she was okay.

I sat there in the sun and watched the people of Millgrove doing their stuff.

Understanding none of it.

It got too much for me to bear alone and, after a while, I went home too.

NEW RULE NUMBER FIVE: You can't go back.

Well, of course you can *physically* go home, I just don't recommend it. It's not good for your sanity to see just how easily you can be painted out of a family picture.

The front door of my house was wide open and the place inside had been systematically trashed.

All the electrical gadgets had been taken out, stripped down, and were probably already being wrecked for parts on the green.

NEW RULE NUMBER SIX: Even to the people you knew and loved it is as if you never existed.

My room was stripped bare.

Stripped right back to the wallpaper.

Nothing of me remained there.

In just a few short hours I had been carefully Photoshopped out of my own family.

Out of my own life.

When I got back downstairs, and when the tears had cleared from my eyes, I found that all of my possessions had been taken down into the back garden and just dumped there.

I think that was the worst moment for me.

Standing there amid the discarded remnants of my life, thinking about the coldhearted programmer who had written the subroutine that got 1.0 parents to empty a forgotten 0.4 son's room, and leave it all piled in the garden like so much rubbish.

I dragged a rucksack out of the debris, filled it with some clothes, books, and mementos from the pile, and then turned my back on the house.

Forever, I thought.

Only thing is: forever is a long, long time.

I went back to the green feeling sick, feeling betrayed, feeling utterly alone. I threaded my way through the crowd of people who no longer knew I had ever existed. They just moved around me without realizing they were doing it. Piling up more gadgets on the green, ready for . . .

For what?

I didn't know.

I was surprised to find Lilly there already. She was almost impossibly relieved to see me and ran over, throwing her arms around me, and crying into my neck.

The story she sobbed into my shoulder was the same as my homecoming, with only minor differences.

She, too, had packed a bag.

"I can't stay here," she said through her tears. "I just can't."

"I know," I said. "I can't either."

We both felt it—the overwhelming need to get away from this place. If we were dead to the people of Millgrove, then it was dead to us. We would be like ghosts haunting our old lives, and if we were going to make it in this world that had forgotten us, we were going to have to do it somewhere other than here.

We stopped round at Kate's house. She and Mr. Peterson had made their decision about how they were going to proceed.

They told us over a breakfast put together from the things in Kate's cupboards. Some toast and cereal, orange juice and hot cup of tea. I ate like I hadn't eaten for a month.

Kate O'Donnell and Rodney Peterson were staying put.

"The truth is I've always been an outsider here," Kate told us. "I don't think things will be that different, if I'm honest. I have Rodney now. We'll be fine."

Mr. Peterson looked over at her and smiled.

They made an okay couple, I thought.

We told them that we understood, said our good-byes, and then Lilly and I set off for Cambridge. The nearest town, a place we both knew, but that wouldn't carry the painful associations of a village that had simply forgotten we ever existed.

It would be a good starting point.

And then, we thought, we would go traveling further.

NEW RULE NUMBER SEVEN: You live with this the best way you can.

CHAPTER 45

And now we're done.

I have made a record of these events and maybe I will feel better for doing it. I feel like I have been carrying all of this around in my head, and it has been weighing me down.

Perhaps the burden will be lighter now.

There are only a few things left for me to say.

No neat, happy ending: but an ending all the same.

There are so many questions that we are unable to answer; but what I can tell you is how we are today.

The 0.4.

In a 1.0 world.

Lilly and I keep moving. It's a choice we made. We decided

that we would see a few places before we decide where we're going to settle and what's going to become of us.

There are a fair few of us 0.4 around, and many of the others we have met are already working on living as closely as they can to how they once did—before this happened. They are busy forming communities, banding together, and generally making the best of the hand that life has dealt us. There are places that the 1.0 don't go—whole estates, whole villages—and the 0.4 move in.

It's easy to find the 0.4 in whatever city or town we visit. Graffiti is our notice board, and we advertise ourselves to others like us; tell each other where we can meet, where we can find beds for the night among friends. We're in this together and, although it is far from perfect, it's far from terrible too.

We stay away from the machines that the 1.0 build. They are forbidden and we know just how we will be rewarded if we dare to break that simple rule.

The 1.0 *love* their gadgets.

They have completely revolutionized the way they live, and have already developed a form of energy that travels through the air and seems to have no environmental impact whatsoever.

To be honest, we mostly stay away from the 1.0 altogether. They are the reminders of everything that we aren't, and of everything we have lost.

In darker moments I wonder how many have gone before

us, previous versions, skipping upgrades and being forgotten by everyone.

Living.

Surviving.

Having families and carrying on their outdated lives.

Generation after generation hanging on, still here, unseen by even the 0.4.

The 0.3.

The 0.2.

The 0.1.

I wonder if they are here too, forgotten as each new version overwrites the old. I wonder if we share this world with the direct descendants of Neanderthals, *Homo erectus,* protohumans. I wonder if they are still here, just hidden from view by the algorithms and code of our programmers.

I think it's likely, but it brings little comfort to know that there are others like us.

If anything, it makes it worse.

We're not unique.

We're just another layer of junk in the landfill of upgraded humanity.

CHAPTER 46

I keep thinking about the night in the barn.

It's like a scab that I keep worrying at with a nail.

I keep thinking about Danny's insistence that the upgrade from 0.4 to 1.0 had been necessary, to stop the human race from destroying itself and the planet it inhabited.

I contrast that with the three things I remember him telling me from the ReadMe file, and think that far from being altruistic, society-improving, humanity-improving god-figures, the programmers responsible for the human upgrade had other things on their minds entirely.

"Fixed system slowdown when individual units are put to sleep, allowing greater access to unconscious processing activity."

"Tightened encrypted storage parameters to comply with new guidelines."

"Completely reworked user interface makes access of data easier and faster."

When the nights are dark and I can't sleep—and those nights are frequent—I often find myself thinking about these improvements, and try to work out just what they say about our programmers, and the programs the 1.0 are running now.

It all comes down to the question of motive.

I think we are *useful* to the programmers.

We are to them as computers are to us.

We are their tools.

The human brain has something like one hundred billion neurons. It's the most sophisticated computer on the planet. Multiply it by the six billion people on Earth and you have a heck of a lot of computing power.

Tie those minds together and you have one hell of a network.

We don't use all of our brains, all of the time. We use the small bits that we need and the rest just sits there. Imagining. Daydreaming. Inventing.

Maybe someone is renting out all that extra processing power.

Or all that extra memory space.

Renting it out from our programmers.

Maybe this is about what most things on our planet are about: commerce.

Maybe we *consumers* are, ultimately, nothing more than *consumables*.

Some of the 0.4 think I'm crazy when I start talking like this, and perhaps I am.

But perhaps I'm not.

Because since the rest of the world was upgraded, all of the 0.4 agree on one, odd, beneficial side effect for us, the ones who missed out.

It's a small comfort, but it's how I have been able to remember so many details when relating these events into a tape recorder.

You see, our memories have become much more effective; the clarity of recollection seems much stronger than before. I remember entire conversations, verbatim passages from books, thoughts I have had and things I have seen, all with such clarity that it's as if, for the first time, we have been allowed to use our whole brains.

Rather than the parts rationed out to us by a memory-intensive operating system.

I guess no one wants to store their data the old way.

CHAPTER 47

Lilly and I eventually came back to Millgrove, to see how our families were doing without us.

Fine but weird is the answer.

I stood in my old home—which no longer looks like the house I grew up in: there are odd tubes and ducts running through the place and the house is lit by, I really can't tell you what by—surrounded by my family, and I was absolutely invisible to them.

They were happy, the three of them, happier than I'd ever seen them. It made me feel angry and sad and confused and alone.

I waited for them all to go out before I dragged the old tape recorder out from under the stairs and . . .

. . . and I guess this is the point where we came in.

Now I have made these tapes, and left a record, Lilly and I are going to travel some more.

Before we set off, there are just two more things for us to do.

First up we're going to look in on Kate O'Donnell and Rodney Peterson, see if they're doing okay, to see if they're still even here.

And then comes the big thing.

The last thing.

We've talked about it, Lilly and me, and it's something that we can't avoid. We have to know. We have to give ourselves the opportunity to make all of this go away.

We're going to stop by the Naylors' silos, and we'll see what happens.

Even if they are still full of the alien programmers' code, we're pretty sure we won't take the upgrade.

But you never know until you are in the position to find out.

That's why we're going to sit there and wait a while.

To see if either of us wants to.

If one of us does, the other will too.

It's our pact.

So this is it. It took a long time to get here, but this is my final message, and the whole reason, I guess, for these tapes.

Lilly and I have talked it over and over, and we agree that the hardest thing about all of this is the fact that we have been forgotten. By our families and friends. By our world.

Everyone of the 0.4 can list the people they have lost and it hurts.

Maybe it shouldn't, but it does.

Hence this testimony.

This recording.

My story.

All our stories.

Our world is the world that exists in the cracks of yours. We can look out through those cracks and see you, but you see us only rarely, out of the corner of your eye, for the briefest of instants, and then we're gone.

When your world moved on, it left us right here.

And you forgot about us.

But.

WE ARE STILL HERE.

Forgotten? Yes.

Unimportant? No.

Because we know the truth about you.

About the way things were.

About the way things changed.

About the way things are.

And we know that everything you are can change in a flash, the next time those alien programmers decide it's time for another upgrade.

Maybe the next upgrade will allow us to be seen, I don't know.

We are safe until then; it seems they don't update dead code.

So, if all the odds against us line up in the right configuration, and if you find this tape, play this tape, and can hear my voice on this tape, then please, just remember we were once here, that we are here now, and that we miss you all.

Farewell.

And.

Please.

Remember.

Us.

AFTERWORD

The Straker Tapes end with that simple plea, an appeal for remembrance. Kyle and Lilly's story ends, and we can only guess at what the future held for them.

Maybe they decided to join us and entered one of the grain silos Kyle describes.

We will never know.

The tapes don't tell us.

If we are to take the story on face value, then we now have answers to questions we didn't even know to ask. And questions we never thought we'd *have* to ask.

So, what about the 0.4?

What can we do for them?

When I was a small boy I used to visit my grandfather in his house in Berkshire. He was a collector of old things. He had a massive hoard of gadgets and trinkets that he really didn't understand, just liked them as objects, as historical monuments to outdated ideas.

He had an old telephone in his collection: a chunky, black thing made out of a mysterious substance called Bakelite. At least it seemed mysterious to me, because it was so unlike the substances we use now.

The telephone used to sit on a stand in the corner of the room in which he stored all of the antique things he had collected.

There was a dial on the front of the telephone, with holes for fingers to turn it, and numbers that you could dial from one to nine, and then a zero.

I used to spin the dial and hold the receiver to my head and it was like a kind of time machine that connected me to the past in a way that felt real and important.

One day I was playing with the telephone and I thought I heard a sound in the earpiece. A distant crackle as if there were a tiny current somewhere along the line. I remember feeling so excited by the sound—which I *had* to be imagining, the phone was not plugged into any network—and I pushed down the buttons on top of the telephone as if that would help to make that crackle clearer.

Of course, pushing the buttons did nothing. I felt frustrated and a little angry. I didn't even realize I was deploying my filaments until they had actually latched onto the mouthpiece of the telephone.

As soon as I noticed what I was doing I recalled them back into my body, but not before they had made an infinitesimal adjustment to the mechanisms of the telephone. I felt scared—my grandfather wouldn't have been pleased to find me tinkering with his antiques—and was about to replace the handset so I could slink away when I heard something.

Something that wasn't a just a distant crackle on a long-dead telephone.

Something that sounded like a human voice, speaking a single word.

I put the receiver back on its cradle and crept out of the room.

I stopped playing with the phone after that. It suddenly scared me.

I never told anyone what I had thought I had heard.

A single word.

It sounded like: *remember.*

Analog equipment, analog people.

When I heard the Kyle Straker tapes for the first time, I found myself thinking about the telephone again. That solitary word: *remember.* Kyle and Lilly begging: *remember us.*

Analog ghost voices from analog equipment.

The 0.4.

The world that once was, which, if Kyle is to be believed, is mere centimeters away from us, separated only by a perceptual filter that weeds out their data and screens it from our senses.

I remembered the telephone and shuddered.

ø ø ø

And that is the reason for this book.

I wanted it out there in the world in a form that the 0.4—if they really exist—could access too.

Analog text for analog people.

If you are reading this, even though the world had moved on and left you behind; if you feel like ghosts haunting this brave new world of ours; if everyone you knew and loved has forgotten you, then I offer this volume as our reply.

I have called it *Human.4*, so that you will know it is about you.

Proof.

We.

Remember.

You.

Mike A. Lancaster,
Editor

RECOVERY SUCCESSFUL.
SOME FILES MAY BE CORRUPTED.

EXCERPT FROM
THE FUTURE WE LEFT BEHIND

DOCUMENT LOADING . . .

Nearly a thousand years have passed since
the recording of the Straker Tapes

. . .

Heisenberg University

Professor Lucas Whybrow
Professor of WorldBrain Studies

The story of Peter Vincent might easily have never been heard. Indeed, it was by pure accident that the flash-memory drive, containing the files and fragments that make up his story, was absorbed into the WorldBrainMass.

The brain's annual growth plan meant that new areas of its underground complex were being claimed as sites for further expansion. These areas, or 'rooms', were flooded with nutrients and new BrainLobes seeded on to them.

Janitor's logs show that the new areas set aside for lobe growth were not properly checked.

I believe that during brain expansion, the data storage unit was absorbed by the young BrainLobes and converted into food, and that Peter Vincent's data entered the BrainMass as a side effect of this process.

I discovered the data, also accidentally. While checking file systems, I came across sectors that seemed out of place and worked for several days to isolate the data; then four months rebuilding them into a file system that I could read.

Corrupt data was then analysed and has been carefully recon-structed using markers I discovered within the Vincent files them-selves.

I am satisfied that the Vincent data I am presenting now is as accurate as it is humanly possible to re-create. I have even included fragments – which are in the form of lists that Peter Vin-cent seemed to like making.

In this record, Peter Vincent speaks of a world that once was and tells a startling story that seems to contain answers to many of the questions we routinely ask ourselves as human beings. It is also flawed and contains errors and gaps that will only open Peter Vincent's story to accusations of fraud and dishonesty.

I will, however, leave you to be the judge.

Recovered Sectors/
File-set 1

"The First Day of My Last Days"

*In extraordinary times, the ordinary takes
on a glow and wonder all of its own.*
Kyle Straker

prologue

File: *224/09/11fin*

Source: *LinkData\LinkDiary\Live\Peter_Vincent\Personal*

<RUN>

. . . Alpha . . .

   . . . I want to tell her that I'm sorry, tell her something for hex sake . . . but the world is ending and this . . . this is all I have left.

   All we have left.

   It . . . I . . . this has all gone badly wrong.

   We are deep underground in these chambers beneath the world we know . . . thought we knew . . . beneath the city and I . . .

   I guess I thought that we had a chance . . . Alpha and me . . . that everything that has happened could still have a happy ending, like in the stories my mother used to tell me.

   It's weird.

   I've been thinking about my mother a lot in the last couple of days. Before all of this, I think I would have found it almost impossible to remember what she looked like without consulting my LinkDiary; now I can see her in my mind plainly, I can remember the sound of her voice as if I was still hearing it.

I remember . . .

<. . . There is a shimmer, like a mirage, a trick of the light, and I am momentarily blinded.

By the time my vision clears, my mother is gone . . .>

Oh.

I'm letting my mind run away with me again, and I haven't got time to let it do that. That's one of the problems with playing around with memories, the wrong ones can bubble up and come into focus at the wrong moment.

I don't even know if that's the actual memory, or my memory of examining that scene later . . . but now I'm really getting ahead of myself.

I don't know if this will be my last diary entry.

I guess it probably will be.

So I need to put a copy of my diary on to an external memory source, because people . . . people need to know. They have to be told. Reminded. Whatever.

I'm having to edit the relevant memory files on the fly; to concentrate on the parts of my daily record that will show the world the truth.

We are in a room full of boxes of useless stuff: relics and papers and an ancient flash drive that I have repaired with my filaments – it should be able to store this data, but I will have to compress the information to fit the limitations of the drive.

I'm sitting here, in the near dark, and I should be talking to Alpha, or holding her, or something like that — but instead I'm hacking into my own memories and editing and copy and pasting, all with my heart beating out of control in my chest while she watches on.

So this is fear. I have to say: I can see why we have strived to eradicate it from our lives.

I'll start shunting the parts I've done on to the memory drive.

The first diary entries — I can't believe it was only three days ago.

Three days?

It feels like a lifetime.

The world has changed . . . is changing . . . and I am the only one who can make a record of the truth.

Here we go . . .

>Deploying filaments . . . <
<DUMP MEMORY>